Rollerball

13 selected stories
by William Harrison

Rollerball

Futura Publications Limited
An Orbit Book

An Orbit Book

First published in Great Britain in 1975
by Futura Publications Limited,
49 Poland Street, London W1A 2LG

Copyright © William Harrison 1966, 1967
1970, 1971, 1972, 1973, 1974

Stories in this volume appeared originally in
the following publications: Cosmopolitan,
Esquire, Mill Mountain Review, New Orleans
Review, Paris Review, Playboy, Saturday Evening
Post, and Works in Progress.

This book is sold subject to the condition
that it shall not, by way of trade or
otherwise, be lent, re-sold, hired out or
otherwise circulated without the publisher's
prior consent in any form of binding or
cover other than that in which it is
published and without a similar condition
including this condition being imposed on the
subsequent purchaser.

ISBN: 0 8600 7865 5

Printed in Great Britain by
Richard Clay (The Chaucer Press), Ltd,
Bungay, Suffolk

Futura Publications Limited
49 Poland Street, London W1A 2LG

This book is dedicated to my father, Samuel Scott Harrison, who refused the pinball machines, and to John Yount, who jumps at me out of the bushes.

Preface

Back in the days when I wrote longhand and concerned myself with the traditional properties of fiction such as characterization, the evocation of setting, and the poetic unities, the world seemed almost to believe in these things with me. In those days I not only kept faith with a few literary standards, but even had the presumption to teach writing to a few nervous students. While this may be possible for me again, I could never do it with a straight face. Nowadays a well-documented Cultural Decline has befallen us and the students in the universities are too depraved to listen to talk of standards and so, I insist, am I.

A long story entitled "A Gentle Hunt," not included here, was my first published work. I had just left theological school (times *have* changed, right?) when I began working on it. After fifteen tortured versions a committee of editors at *The Saturday Evening Post* accepted it—and not knowing how long I had struggled against cliché with that title printed it as "A Man of Passion." These editors loved my sentimental period and published "The Pinball Machines," a kindly story about my father, and several other stories before rejecting "The Hermit." They suggested that story needed heavy revision, imagining, I feel sure, that the Stream of Consciousness might be a creek where I liked to go fishing in Montana.

Certainly, after the lyrical meadows of "The Hermit," I went into the dark woods. Yet I feel compelled to admit that, personally, and contrary to considerable current literary opinion, I don't feel the more experimental and embittered last pieces have any more intrinsic value than some of my earlier and more frankly sentimental ones.

The past, though perhaps somewhat uncompleted, is mostly itself; the present is always zany and elusive; and the future, maybe, is a game of Roller Ball Murder.

But I don't mean to be apocalyptic.

Many of our commercial and critical propagandists—who are perhaps close enough to be nearly indistinguishable now—insist that the short story is, like the novel or the word itself, dead. This is big prophecy and heavy stuff. Like all propagandists, they want nothing less than to address the whole culture with their opinions. Most of life, though, is lived and understood at a less public frequency—filled with small griefs, joys, ironies, absurdities, and pains. And that's how the story testifies. Unlike the major sociological observation and even unlike the big novels, say, which call attention to themselves and their World View, the story sneaks in a few microcosmic truths. At times, its focus is frightfully small and its meaning frightfully large. And, whatever, even without that claim, the story, like the poem, is a humble package. The author of the story knows this and derives considerable pleasure from this fact; he is a miniaturist—with all the minor and subversive enjoyments of that role—and he sets a small hieroglyph against the armor of the body politic.

Enough, though. Enough. The claim of humility, as you will see with my fireman, is a wicked boast itself.

Contents

The Warrior (1971)   15
The Hermit (1968)   25
Down the Blue Hole (1973)   44
Eating It (1970)   56
The Pinball Machines (1968)   64
Roller Ball Murder (1973)   77
The Blurb King (1971)   96
A Cook's Tale (1966)   104
The Arsons of Desire (1972)   130
The Good Ship Erasmus (1971)   145
Under the House (1972)   160
Nirvana, Götterdämmerung,
    and the Shot Put (1972)   171
Weatherman: A Theological Narrative (1973)   183

ROLLER
BALL
MURDER

The Warrior

When I served in the American army my trick was crawling by a sentry in the dark of night. No one was ever better at it: inching along, scarcely breathing, rippling a muscle here or shoving off gently there so that my body sometimes passed at an enemy's very feet in the good strong shadows of a moonless watch. I've passed a man so close that he could have turned and stepped on me, in which case, of course, he would never have taken another step. This was my specialty, getting by a man this way, and I did it in Korea and later when I wasn't an American anymore—just one of the world's mercenaries as I am now—in Algiers, the Congo, Biafra, and so on.

Africa, lovely restless continent, is just out that way across the water. This is my home now, this little port, Javea, and if you look out from our hill you can see the beach, Cabo de San Antonio, with the lighthouse, the city and mountain beyond it. Being just across from Africa this way pleases me and lately I've considered going back over with El Fatah, say, or even the Israelis if they'd give me a good platoon which they probably wouldn't. Spain is fine, but it reeks of peace now; not that I don't enjoy it with my family here, but before too long I always start contacting old friends in the business or reading the classified sections again, seeing who wants a warrior this season. One job of mine came right out of the London *Telegraph* and another I got out of *France Soir*. Always in Africa: that old dark continent over there where a good savage is always appreciated.

This is my villa, all paid for, my pool, over there the vineyard and terraced olive grove. We sit here in the *naya* in the evenings, my wife, Val, and I, and drink these good local wines and repeat the old stories; I'm not one of those who can't talk about battles or the things that go on during a good fight. My daughters, Jenny and Kip, sleep just above us in their own rooms. You've seen the antiques in the house, the gardens, the Porsche and Rover, my motorbikes: you know we have a good life here. This is a nice place, better in climate than Southern California, say, where I've lived, or the Riviera—which gets too cold for me in the winter. It's just that I get restless, as I say, and of course it was much better here on the Costa Blanca a few years back before the tourists found us, before the entrepreneurs— there's this queer film festival down on the beach right now—and before the big contractors moved in and started building these cut-rate villas. This part of the hillside twenty years ago was all fruit trees, lovely; that was when I came here, when I was in my twenties just after Korea and hard as an oak and just a mean kid.

Val sits there in the cool afternoon breeze reading about the film festival in the provincial newspaper. She told me they're having one Fellini, one Mike Nichols, and the rest of the movies are by Frenchmen: Christ, some show. The kids and tourists have been in town for days, sprawling out on the sand down there, eating paella at our beach restaurants. Look at my wife: quiet, that good Spanish profile, still with me. My heartsblood. We have a generation of naked little flower girls now, not a woman among them like my Val.

This is the arsenal, yes, and everything's about ready. A solid room: these old tiles make a fine echo when you walk on them. The sound—I've thought about this some —lends a little importance to every movement made in here. These are the automatic weapons, here are the mortars and a few heavier pieces, over there the explosives—some of which, I admit, I confiscated from the local *Guardia Civil*. I sat at this table and filled all these cartridges myself. Everything is sorted out and inspected and I've confiscated a boat, too—I'll tell you about all this later—and I have a motorbike and car waiting in strategic spots. No one suspects a thing. I'm still a man who can slip by in the darkness.

Sit here on the *naya*.

Get us some drinks, okay, Val, baby?

We should have a long talk and I should explain a lot of myself to you, but of course there isn't time for much of that. This domestic life—let me say this much— is great when I come back from assignments. We water ski, skin dive along the reef, go over to the club for tennis in the late afternoons. But after a few weeks shadows start coming over me and let's face it: there isn't anything here that measures up to crawling by a guard in the darkness or running headlong into an attack. Not that we should get too philosophical, but paradise is a moody place. I get into the glooms, then, and start sitting around my table in the arsenal drinking and reading. Oh sure, you saw all the books inside the house: I'm no brute.

What will really come after nationalism—have you thought about it? As I see it, this tribalism will eventually go away, and, no, not because of the United Nations, noble though the effort is. The UN is just a referee among the nations, after all, and so basically approves of the spirit of nationalism. No, big business will take over the masses. Men's loyalties in the next century or two, in my view, will shift from France and Pakistan and Brazil to Olivetti, Westinghouse, and Shell Oil. The big corporations are already cutting across borders. And government—think how obvious this is—will become a kind of regulation agency which will determine when the big corporations are cheating and when they're not. Clandestine business—war of sorts, yes—will go on. But men won't finally be as emotional about products and companies—especially if they can change jobs easily, after all—as they are about their homeland. Things will settle down and my sort should eventually become obsolete.

But make no mistake about it, eh: we're not obsolete yet, are we? And war is still a great education in reality—the way things really are. The kids on the beach need to learn that lesson; they nourish a lot of vague hopes, unaware.

Ah, thanks, Val. Sit here with us.

Civilization has been a long breeding process, true, but we aren't all bred and civilized yet, so there's the gap between our hope for ourselves and what really is. The warrior is out of favor nowadays, for instance, because so many people imagine that it's surely time for him to be finished. But that's hardly realistic with new nations still emerging, guerrilla wars, protest movements flaring up. The old warrior should be given his due. Ah, let me tell you, I dream now and then, you know, and shadows come over my sleep, names and faces swimming up inside me: Marathon, Alexandria, Hastings, Lyons. Does any of this make sense? Sometimes I feel that I just got back from, say, Dunkirk—or Okinawa. I've had strange dreams for months and when I wake up—the really curious part is this—I'll know how to work a crossbow or I'll remember a particular coat of mail I've worn with blue ringlets. And I forget my rank—have I just been a captain, a foot soldier?—and once I turned to Val and said, hey, remember how we walked out of the trees at Shiloh and found that road and made it up toward the next town with our wounded, and she gave me this odd look. Val indulges me; we've been together a long time and naturally she knows the humor I've been in lately.

You came here wanting to know what I'm going to do, I realize, and I'm going to tell you. Perform my art: that's all. It's partially for the old shell-shocked ego and self-satisfaction, sure, and you can invent your own explanations—such as, oh well, he never had any sons and this is part of his masculine anxiety and that sort of thing. Whatever, I'm going to show some of my repertoire of moves; the old ballet master will rise up and dance—while you stay up here, naturally, with Val. But it won't be *just* to demonstrate my skills. My attack will be a lesson in history. If everything goes right—and it will—I'll kill a thousand of the unwary this evening; I'll be identified, of course, and someone reading tomorrow morning's news will decipher some of the meaning of it all.

Some ice? No, my limit's one this afternoon.

Listen to me, where is history? My notion is that the philosophers can never tell us—nor the artists or anyone else. They can only record things static and gone while the world nowadays powers along at an overwhelming speed. Only speed and power themselves are listened to: things that zoom and explode beyond our immediate comprehension like comets so that we stop and ask, "Hey, what was that?" All lessons now must be actions: scars that wound the world's face so that it can never quite forget. And there's an irony here you ought to consider: it turns out that I'm one of the great humanitarian instructors, saying, Wake up, see that you're still in a twilight of barbarism, be ready! It's a tough truth to take, but valuable—far better for mankind than so much idle wishing about its nature.

Well, you should know. This evening I'll attack the film festival. All those passive onlookers down there on the beach. They're down there pondering their various apocalyptic films, conning themselves with art and sand, imagining they're seeing something important flicker in front of their eyes. They're zombies, those hip children, passing love messages around. It's not that I hate them—I have no particular intolerance for one lifestyle or another—it's just that, oh, I don't flatter myself here either, I'm their instructor. I hope you can glimpse what I mean: time is against them, they don't know where they are, their fantasy is a dream of death.

Look at this view. A few sails out there on the bay this afternoon. I'll hate leaving here, but Val will join me, naturally, and there'll be many more days like this. We may live in Istanbul—I was there once years ago, I forget exactly when.

You'll want to know exactly how it will be. All right, I'll come down from the rocks so that I can sweep the whole beach before me. There should be about a thousand bathers, another thousand gathering inside the canopy to watch that stupid promoter—he calls himself an impresario—unwind his dull films. Weighted down with ammo, I won't move fast—I won't have to. When I open fire, I'll just get some astonished looks. You odd little soldier, they'll be thinking before they die, you're all baggy with packs and weapons and you rattle when you walk and look silly. Their eyes will fill up with hurt, then, and I'll just move through them; strangely enough, it will take several minutes before they even start running ahead of my fire. A big Scandinavian girl will be blown right out of her bikini, and if you had the right mind about it the sight would strike you funny: zap, she's undressed, flying off in a little slow-motioned erotica. One brave idiot will come at me with a rubber float after he's wounded; oh, please, don't hit me with that, and I'll cut him in two. A group of rowdies, their motorcycles there beside them in the sand, boys in their marbled T-shirts and girls lying on towels with their halters loosened: I'll empty on them at very close range because they're too cool to move. Almost casually, now, I sweep down the beach, walking near the surf where the sand is packed underfoot, spraying my fire into the wall of bodies just ahead. They start to fall over each other now as I step into a sand castle and advance. No time to finish the wounded, but surprisingly there aren't many of those. Under the canopy just ahead the crowd begins to stir, but by this time I stop, set up my mortar and lob a few shells—first just beyond them and then into the tent itself. Human parts everywhere: our beach runs a little red now. As they race toward me in confusion and away from those first volleys, I let go with the remainder of my .50-caliber material. This turns them back again, and now I have the crowd on the run. Heavy ammo mostly gone, I leave weapons and empty cartridge belts and become more mobile. I carry the mortar only a few more quick meters toward the flaming canopy, let fly a few more lobs in the direction of the beach restaurants—a skillet, a Fanta sign, a Cinzano bottle high in the air—then leave the mortar, too. Our impresario steps out on stage in front of a camera, and I give him the first voice of the burp gun;

he and his camera dissolve, film cascading out into a strange and shiny black flower among the ruins. In a hurry, I move out again, calculating my minutes. The local police force—seven white cheerful uniforms, three pistols, four whistles strong—should be arriving in the next five minutes, so I dash toward my screaming crowd once more. Two grenades: they turn like wild horses, stampeding over each other, some of them diving off into the canal where the boats for the hotel are at dock. I burp a few volleys into them, they turn again. With my .45 in hand and the burp gun strung on my shoulder, I start my last run. A Spanish kid with his spearfishing gun advances on me and with my .45 I amputate his right leg. Spare the brave in heart. Reaching my motorbike with one twilight hour left and work to do, I start up the main road toward the village, cut across a field, join another smaller country road, and hurry toward the charges I've planted. By this time the *Guardia Civil* scurries around, each man inside the armory searching for his rifle, shouting orders at the next man; the captain talks to the police commissioner on the telephone. Great confusion: they speculate on how many men attacked the beach and port and whether or not this is a communist or loyalist uprising. Meanwhile, I set the fuse on the armory, pausing there at the rear of the building, my motorbike leaning against the white stucco wall. An old man passes on his mule-drawn cart, nodding at me and smiling. Then I move on, two blocks away to the school—which is empty, naturally, but which will occupy the citizens when it, too, goes up. Here I drop the motorbike—some crafty policeman probably spotted me on it as I headed away from the beach—and in an MG which I recently confiscated in Alicante I start driving back to my carnage. Keeping my grenades, the burp gun, and my .45, I shuck off the recognizable fatigues which I wore during the beach extravaganza. As I drive slowly along, the concussion of my plastic explosives thuds throughout the valley and mushrooms of gray smoke dot the village. At the port everyone still runs amok. Mothers are crying out names and one of my enemies, a white-frocked policeman with a silver whistle, directs traffic from his usual position beside the fountain in the square. Coasting through the congestion, I honk. Spaniards and tourists move courteously aside. I muse about the town, my Javea: the village up there on the hill was built first away from the sea so that pirates would be discouraged from attacking. Later, in our century when such precaution wasn't necessary, the town grew down toward the harbor. Incredible. At the port, I pull back the rayon coverlet on my waiting cabin cruiser. All is ready: food, the radio and radar set, enough armament to take on anything at sea. I work leisurely, starting the engines, as off in the distance columns of smoke rise up evenly from the village. Four or five shots ring out and one wonders what they're firing at or who is left to shoot? For a moment, then, my dreams overtake me and I'm somewhere else; voices of hundreds rise off a plain, the cry of a long charge, and I'm there, yet not. Revving up, I cast off and smoothly set forth into the canal. A final gesture now: I deposit my last grenades in the docked cruisers as I pass. One goes up in a ball of pleasant fire, then another, another, and I roar into the bay without one parting shot to protest my exit. From the hillside, secure, Val—and you—can see my departure. Everything goes as planned, and I am adream; names flutter in my thoughts, many names of comrades and victims, and I see a castle on a distant promontory flying a single black flag, the body of a friend—dressed as a legionnaire—swollen in the desert, a smiling Asian boy armed only with a sharp stick.

All this will happen.

Africa, gleaming under starlight now, awaits us. In Cairo later, at the Ding Dong Bazaar, Val will join me and we'll have a drink at a sidewalk table, hold hands, and talk about you and others. I'll eventually be at work again, inching by a man as he sleeps on his rifle at an outpost, scouting a jungle camp, sighting an enemy in my scope, instructing the innocents.

The Hermit

He fled to a deserted ranch up in the Flathead country of Montana, to a desolation of old log buildings in the high timber country beyond Columbia Falls, beyond the Polebridge Store on the North Fork near the Canadian border. The ranch had once belonged to his father, but now the heavy winter snows and the frenzies of wandering bears had left the lodge and outbuildings lonely and ravished. Rubble, all of it, but a sturdy rubble: the great logs—so large that a man's arms couldn't encircle one—stood as heavy and as bold as pyramids. In spite of the snows, then, and the furious summer weeds, the ranch was still intact when old Ossinger arrived.

He took up residence in the south wing of the lodge in the late summer, rebuilt the main fireplace, and shoveled out silt and broken glass from the huge rooms. No one remarked on his presence except Gammon, the mailman, and Cone, the storekeeper. Every Tuesday Gammon picked up the hermit's nearly illegible grocery list from the large wooden box with the heavy leather straps which stood at the main gate. On Wednesday, after Cone had filled the list at his store, Gammon delivered the hermit's weekly supply of groceries. Ossinger would lift his load onto his back and shuffle down that rough mile of road into the ranch. The gate remained closed and no one ventured in, and soon the peak of Mt. Kintla was patched with snow and the frosted pine needles cracked underfoot as Ossinger made his Wednesday pickup. Then winter completed his isolation; tons of snow sealed him off and he was forgotten until spring.

On the cold winter mornings which followed, Ossinger stood in the ruins of that vast ranch—his father had built it in hopes of turning it into a speakeasy resort with jazz bands and skiing and private planes on a runway in the east meadow—trying to decipher the world into which he had come. He read the elusive script of nature: the strange markings left by stags on the trunks of the pines, the glossy hieroglyphics of a snail's path across the stones of the river. In those long winter evenings he sometimes added his own slanting handwriting to that mystic alphabet around him: clumsy sentences composed in the glow of his massive hearth. He struggled to read, to comprehend, to add his signature to those encompassing him. Time was a great tablet, he sensed, on which all living creatures scribbled, and though the language of this place was obscure and confounding, he kept trying to see it. He grew hypnotic, dazed, visionary. In the mornings, wrapped in a blanket in that immense main room of the lodge, racked with hunger, his arms and legs shivering, his eyes would narrow and glaze; he would suddenly peer into the patterns of a bird's frail, small scratchings in the snow of the window ledge. "Let me see," he'd whisper to the gaping room around him. Or he'd touch the delicate braille of the frost on the window itself, and summon all his will to know. Finally, overcome by cold and hunger, he'd build his fire, stir up a small pot of coffee, and open his cupboard. But by noon, often, his trance would return. The winter passed; though at its mercy, he survived.

He appeared at the Polebridge Store in late March and his odor filled the room like the sour musk of a wet bear. Cone, the storekeeper, left the door open although snow blew around their feet from the porch. Ossinger loaded his box with gear: two traps, two fly rods, lures, a net, a six-inch knife, three pans, then enough staples to bring its weight to more than a hundred pounds. Then he pulled from his old coat a book of checks and wrote out payment in full; the bank was the First Federal of Chicago. While Cone inspected it, Ossinger jerked his straps into place, hoisted the box to his back, and started out. "You're not carryin' that no eight miles when I got a good truck sitting out back!" Cone called after him. But Ossinger didn't acknowledge him.

Moments later Cone's new Dodge pulled up beside Ossinger on the road. The storekeeper swung the door open. Ossinger stopped and looked at him, then gazed up at the gathering swirls of snow, then unloaded his burden into the back of the truck and climbed atop it. They drove up the North Fork road to Ossinger's gate where he jumped down from the truck and shouldered the box again.

"I'll drive you all the way," Cone said. "Let me."

"Nobody can come in," Ossinger told him.

Exasperated, Cone looked at him and said, "Hell, man, you're crazy," then turned the truck around and headed back.

Insane, insane. The melting spring snows boomed down every crevice in the mountains; the high winds started, causing hideous blowdowns along the ridges, whipping the pines around the ancient ranch until they sang a high and bedeviled music into Ossinger's ears. Insane, they whispered, and he couldn't argue with them, for he continued to read the elements and creatures of his place as though they really had something to say; *the spider is a mathematician, his web a signature of order; the beaver is an engineer, and he makes a watery wall of China; the mosquito autographs my kneecap; the loon is a singer; the eagle decorates the sky with his transient dives and arches.*

Do they say anything, Ossinger wondered, except their own names? Is there love among them and do they want to communicate with one another and their universe? Or do they simply mark the world with their separate vanities? And am I mad to keep asking, to keep reading, to keep pondering their codes?

Cone stood behind his counter that spring thinking about the hermit and consequently about himself.

Those who came to the North Fork country nowadays, he reminded himself, have two houses, often three, and they come on vacation to glance up idly at Kintla, to fish in Hay Creek and the river, and they abandon nothing of an old life. They're tourists buying a change of scene—even the ones who spend the summers—and they go back to office politics and city money. On paper, they own the whole Flathead country. A lawyer in Idaho, a teacher in New Jersey, a young banker in Oklahoma: each imagines that he owns a place up here. Not true, though, Cone knew. Standing behind his counter, he thought of Ossinger: the only man in three decades to begin in this wild country as he, Cone, had done.

Cone was deliberately enigmatic. He had lived his

life as a friendly storekeeper, always good-natured and neighborly, but he kept his reserve, always hiding more than he shared of himself, and this had become a source of personal power and vitality for him. When he talked —because of this reserve—other men listened. Often, somewhat cleverly, he allowed someone to imagine that he had offered them the secret of himself; he seemed to wink at them and silently present them with the key to his inner life. He never actually did this, but allowed first one neighbor, then another, to imagine it—which increased his power even more than a natural austerity might have done. Every man in the North Fork felt that he knew Cone best, yet when they talked among themselves his neighbors admitted that Cone was a mystery, a curious pleasure in their midst.

He was a reader of books, and his interests were, in order, studies of the female nude, history, supernaturalism, and the birds of North America. He had two shelves of erotica, more than a hundred book club selections in history and wildlife, and the major texts of clairvoyance and the occult. He sat every evening in the big Morris chair by his cookstove in the back of the store and read his books and newspapers—he had no radio—until he fell asleep and his hand dangled off the arm of the chair and touched the head of his collie bitch, Jenny, who slept on the floor beside him. Eventually Jenny would nudge him and he would get up and go to bed. He would lie in his bunk, then, surrounded by his frayed volumes. The books of nude studies had collected since his wife's death; supernaturalism had originally been her interest, which accounted for that; history had been Cone's father's passion; the wildlife books had come to the shelves almost by necessity— because Cone had to know what he looked at. There were also six novels, all by Zane Grey, and a book of poems by Robert Frost, his wife's favorite. At times, adream in his bunk, his books, his customers, and his dead wife would float behind his eyes; and in the mornings, positioned behind his counter, he'd long to say something important to his first customer—just to hear himself utter it—but, of course, he'd keep his reserve.

When Cone went down to Kalispell at the end of the month, he didn't cash Ossinger's check with the others, but instead asked his bank to write to Chicago, to ask about the account, and, if possible, to run a credit check on his new neighbor. He felt uncomfortable doing it, but couldn't help himself. Then, back at his store, waiting for the report, he could only know what the old man put into his belly: the pork and beans, salted crackers, canned meat, potatoes. He could only talk to Gammon while he waited, asking, "Is he out on the road waiting when you deliver to him on Wednesdays?"

"Never," Gammon told him. "Oh, he might be off in the woods, waitin' for my truck, but he don't show his face. Too proud to let me see him pickin' up that box of vittles, I reckon."

Ossinger: a German name. Probably a madman, a lunatic, Cone decided. The old man's smell seemed to linger in the store, and soon, at night, the pages of Cone's book seemed to blur before his eyes, and he strained to recall what the old ranch looked like—he had been on the property six or seven times—and to imagine how Ossinger managed. That was it: how could a man manage absolutely alone? Cone was struck with a curious jealousy; he was provoked, agitated, and felt, somehow, outdone, and couldn't help speculating about everything: how does he cut his wood and haul it? does he keep trot lines? has he started rebuilding the whole place or does he live like a pig in one of those rotting rooms? how? what sort is he?

On a sudden warm day in early April the letter came. Ossinger enjoyed good but unestablished credit. His bank account was in order. He had been in prison for thirty years.

"That," said Cone, slapping the letter against his thigh, "is just exactly what I thought! Something like that anyway! Just what I thought!"

That summer the tourists poured into the North Fork, spilling across the Polebridge from Glacier Park, coming up for picnics and fishing from Columbia Falls. One evening a float party stopped on the gravel bar at Ossinger's place, half a mile from his lodge; they cooked a meal, pitched their tent, sang songs until midnight, and in the morning left beer cans and paper strewn around. Ossinger went down after they were gone, gathered the trash and burned it. The water glistened, excited him, and he spent the remainder of the day fishing and walking along the river. He caught one bull trout, a mean, old, yellowed six-pounder, and he gazed into its pale and empty eye as if some fierce prophecy hid in it. Then he threw it back, watched it knife away. At late evening, tired, he cut across the peninsula of thick woods to a cluster of rocks farther down the river on his property; web and moss reached out and touched him as he made his way through the new underbrush. Then he watched his gray hackle drift on the ripple, bob, and saw the flashing sides of the rainbow which took it. Nature is metaphor, he told himself, and I am a landscape.

He slept deeply that night, until a noise outside the lodge the next morning waked him. From the window he saw a young couple. Their Jeep was no more than twenty feet from his front porch and they were talking to each other with great excitement; the girl was plainly exhilarated by his place, and she spun around, her bright orange skirt billowing around her brown legs, and her voice was innocent and full of laughter. A few moments later, dressed, Ossinger stood on his porch before them.

"Who in the world *are* you?" the girl asked, breathlessly. "And what is this place?"

"The gate on the road was closed," Ossinger said. Though he tried to deliver this line sternly, he smiled.

"If you *live* here, sir, then we're sorry," the boy said.

"I do live here," Ossinger said. "And the name of the ranch is Limbo. And the ground you stand on is haunted, all full of bones and time. You can look inside the lodge just for a minute, but then you'll have to go."

"We don't want to bother you," the boy answered.

"How you talk!" the girl exclaimed, laughing and unafraid, and she took her boyfriend's hand and led him onto the porch. "He said we could look inside! Come on!"

They entered his door and saw the great vacant rooms, rafters menacing in the shadows above them, the large, single chair draped with skins in front of the hearth; the room was cool and ancient, like a cavern. When the young couple turned, Ossinger had left them alone.

Loneliness is pure, he wanted to tell them, *but vain like everything else. This is my place and the gate is shut, and those who trespass here are the curious ones, those who come to find me, and curiosity is a form of love and communication, a gentle touch that doesn't bruise or break the skin.*

"Hellooo-oh!" they called, but he watched them from

an upstairs window without answering. They closed the gate behind them when they left, and that afternoon at the Polebridge Store they told Cone what had happened, what the old man had said to them.

Cone began to think about the hermit again after that, in spite of the heavy summer business, the traffic in his store, the lost travelers. When, after Jenny had thrown her third litter, one of the puppies turned out exceptionally strong and full in the chest, Cone decided to put it into the grocery delivery.

"Maybe he don't want no dog," Gammon objected.

"We'll see about it," Cone answered.

"Shouldn't you put in a note, too?"

"No, just the pup."

"I'm not even sure this is with postal regulations," Gammon said, placing the animal inside the cardboard box next to the cornmeal.

"Who the hell said you're a postman?" Cone asked, grinning. "Aren't you just my grocery boy, mine and that old coot's? Make your delivery."

The gift was never acknowledged and Cone wondered, then, among other things, what had happened to his big male pup. He brooded until August. Then Gammon came up with his brother-in-law one weekend for a float trip on the river and they asked Cone to join them; they planned to go up to the border and float back to the store, and since they'd float by Ossinger's ranch, Cone agreed to go.

En route from the border they took several grayling and a few trout and whitefish, stopping at every likely looking gravel bar for the enthusiastic brother-in-law. He was a tall boy, a young schoolteacher with a gold tooth. Finally they went by Ossinger's place and Cone strained to see something; the old buildings occasionally

winked into sight beyond the pines. "Over here! Pull
over here!" Cone shouted, when they had almost gone
past.

Silence descended around them as they fished from
Ossinger's gravel bar. The nearby woods were dark
blue, full of the lush summer undergrowth which curled
at the feet of a few tamaracks which rose up like spec-
ters. Cone listened, but heard nothing. Then, while his
companions fished, he climbed the path for a better
look. Beyond the meadow he saw the old lodge and six
outbuildings, like a holy ruin, all of it, rotting and
splendid. His eyes narrowed. His curiosity was almost
painful—a gnawing in his chest—but he returned to the
rubber raft. The brother-in-law was holding a trout
beside his face, posing for a photograph.

September again. Cone's preoccupation with Ossinger grew. Twice he rode the mail route with Gammon, ostensibly to talk, though Gammon was a dull
conversationalist, a man who liked football too much
every autumn. Then one day Cone enclosed two books
in the grocery delivery, one of his ornithic picture
books and the journals of Lewis and Clark by DeVoto.
After a week he received no response.

By this time he had devised a character for Ossinger:
another lonely intellectual, one of those tormented academic types who frequently invaded the North Fork, a
man cynical toward Western technology. Cone would
stand behind his counter, sigh, and wonder how many
subjects Ossinger could be authoritative about. A week
passed and he sent two more books, a novel from his
book club and one of his photography anthologies with
only a few nudes. He waited for an answer, again, in
vain. Then, once more, he became self-critical. Am I, he
asked himself, just a fake? Living up here on the fron-

tier: is that just pretense? I'm probably just a storekeeper, mercantile and corrupted, and not what I've imagined at all. He gazed up at the bright red and white cans of soup and felt, because of Ossinger, like a drugstore cowboy, an imposter and a sham.

Yet he fought off his impulses to go and see the hermit. He remained guarded, a man closed like a fist against all sentimentalities. He had practiced a life of caution, after all, and had deliberately tried to make a riddle of himself and to hoard his personal feelings. And isn't that, he wondered, what a man is: the reticent creature, a thing born to be tucked into itself, an inscrutable beast, too, taught by every society to endure pain and anxiety in a silence which could be interpreted as strength? He knew that he wanted to visit Ossinger, that he wanted to walk down that road into the old man's ranch, shake hands, talk with him about the Flathead country, about growing old and the ways of the world which they had both abandoned. I'm sixty years old, he wanted to say, and you're older than that, Ossinger, and time bullies us, but we fight madness, not death, and we understand paradoxes, too, especially that a man often struggles against loneliness by isolating himself. He wanted to tell Ossinger this and much more, about the old days on the North Fork, about his wife's death. Let us devise our fatal calendar together, he also wanted to say. Let us be friends—on our own terms, of course.

But he wouldn't go. Instead, when the first snows wafted down from the mountains in October, he sent two more books. Then, on the Wednesday before Thanksgiving, he added a small turkey to Ossinger's grocery order with a note indicating that he was doing this for all his regular customers. A lie, naturally, but he didn't care. He hid the items down in the bottom of the cloth sack so that Gammon wouldn't see them.

Ossinger, asleep in his stinking blankets, listened to the sound of another winter.

Nature: does it ever write in a language of love or is it the alien and neutral scrawl? Birds, descend on my porch. Sing. Talk to me. Bears, poor, shy friends, linger here. The snows are coming to shut us off again. I watched the puppy die. Distemper. His hind legs weakened and he sprawled and bumped and tumbled after me, sliding on my father's floors, wanting, I believe, to sleep in the pulse of my hand. His head nodded at the last, twitched and rolled, and his eyes went out before his last breath. A puppy in my food box. A message from you, Cone, and did I, I asked myself, have to depend on another person? Or is the sky infinite with milk? Can the trees transform me? Can I become a leaf and will the seasons translate my isolation?

Books, you gave me then. The prison library: rows of molded encyclopedias, stacks of National Geographic, Bibles and religious pamphlets, some hundred volumes in all. I read them every one in the second year. I spent the first in disbelief. Turned dumb after that, turned sexless, went mad and betrayed. Books in my food box. I read with a slow fingernail.

My wife, Cone, held her breasts to my lips. The honeyed nipples. Thighs to addle you, slim as those in the photographs you sent, all white, all silk. The memo of sex: misplaced and lost. Betrayed by a kiss, a torso, a friend too weak for my friendship. I killed them both, old storekeeper, and misplaced the wondrous memo, and failed to tell you about it while you watched me prowl your shelves. Her hair—did I tell you even this?—grew in the coffin and cushioned her, wrapped her round, then, lovely brown stuff, choked her soul. Doing life, I dreamed of it. Doing life which was never singular, for I was at least two young men and three old ones those years.

I lie here in hibernation with the facts of myself: divorced from my childhood by time, divorced from Chicago by space, divorced from a wife by murder. One year I befriended the Negro, but he killed his cellmate. Two years I worked in the infirmary. Complaints every day from the men whose lives had become sores. Another year learning leatherwork. My teacher paroled, at last, leaving behind a room of scraps, shoestrings, mistakes. And all the years, storekeeper, her hair encompassed her in the grave, hair wet with my kisses. Observe the leaf, its veins exposed: a small hopeful hand meant to catch the raindrop, a servant of the elm. Observe the fossils in my river rocks: dumb notations eternity will never read. Clearly, a person very much like myself did a terrible act, but after such a long homage to guilt, what then? My father, old rube, old dreamer, is long dead. His last poker hand pays the yearly taxes on this ungainly ranch, provides my refuge. My kin is gone, conceded to the elements in Ohio, Florida, Illinois. No sons. No friend with whom I once drank beers, talked books, shot snooker, dreamed vocations: his name yellows in a forgotten headline, his bones are chalk.

I've spent two silly days hauling colored rocks from the river, encircling my lodge with them, enjoying their dazzle. The flow of the river, old storekeeper, flows in me, and the rocks, thrown down like mystic runes around my house, guard my sleep. Odor of pine. Sharp ax. And, in strange moments, the aurora borealis. No mistake in coming here, old storekeeper; I am awed, and awe—a lost and holy emotion—cleanses me.

Kneeling, Ossinger laced his boots. Drawing on his mackinaw, he wondered about the depth of the snow on the main road. Eight long miles. He stepped onto his porch as a hawk spiraled above him in the cold sky.

Homage to guilt, yes, but when does a debt end? Guilt is so time-consuming, dear sender of turkeys, and soon I should probably build the ranch. Rent the pasture to cattle, watch them graze. Putty the windows, calk the doors, sweep and polish. Will young, bright girls come, then, to fill the meadows with laughter? Or a widow, perhaps, slim and gray with a mouth sweet as cloves who will read the ranch and sleep in the crook of my arm for one night or forever? Or will an old man, a brother, stroll down this road, my crude food box on his back, smiling, with whiskey and news and weather talk and a glimpse of my sorrow?

With a grunt Ossinger lifted his empty food box onto his shoulders and turned toward Polebridge. His knees pumped high in the snowdrift until he reached the tire treads in the road. *Gammon's path.* His thumbs wedged in the straps, loosening the bite of the leather through his coat. *Two miles then rest awhile,* he decided. He didn't think about the return trip.

Last winter loneliness piled up in drifts around my lodge. Some days I stayed in bed, listened to the wind, wolves, small scratchings, the rumble of my own belly, the creakings of the rooms. On such days the soup froze at the hearth and the forests filled with ghosts, whirlwinds of sleet, and to rise, to pad across the cold floor, was an act of will, an affirmation. Sleep in those foul blankets, odd dreamer, and never rise: the thought occurred to me. Suicide. The final homage. But I finally jumped out to blow on the stale ashes, to kindle the fire, lace my boots, cover my ears, tote my food box. Suffered hallucinations, yes, but damned if I'd embrace

*the bed forever. On the road one morning I saw myself
lurking behind a pine; he was slightly older, perhaps,
somewhat less erect with manikin hands, but with my
same brow and scrawny neck, and he shuffled behind
me as I picked up my food. Not there now, no. But
there he was, marrow of my marrow, his breath asteam,
his footfall crackling after mine. Or one night, sitting
warm in my chair and needing logs, my hands became
transparent and I watched the blood pulsing around
the tips of my fingers like an endless, slow locomotive.
Wrote it down in my diary. And who will read me when
I'm gone and my words are finally punctuated? The
book will turn into pastel cheese for the rats of the
ranch, and they'll eat it and grow wise. Last winter:
ah, neighbor, my own self-inflicted confinement at last.
Blizzards of days. My hands chapped, broke open and
bled.*

*Of course Lewis and Clark, thank you, shot the
rapids, went down with fever, took lovemaking disease
from the indians. The frontier, neighbor, is a fragile
thing; push on it and it breaks, spills like Atlantis into
the twisted waters of history, never recovered. Of course
those pioneers saw the plumage of North America, too,
thank you again, Cone, and the eagle watched itself
being watched. And they dreamt of slender naked girls
in their nightbags. Thanks for those. Books: they made
books out of wind-waving grass. My eyes have dimmed
by firelight; thanks for the eyestrain, but I'm buying
kerosene this time and is that what you wanted? My
money after all? Passing the logging road now where
the devil-eyed drivers go hopping downstate, down-
world, taking the curves with their chains banging. The
logging road and the community meeting hall. I'm halfway, neighbor, and the tracks widen.*

A cabin along the road struck out of log. Fancy a

family living there, four children, all dirty, very poor. Initials cut into that tamarack, some thin nick which becomes a scar wide as the trunk, deep as the furrows of a face. A young man returns to find his beginnings, looks for his landmark tree, but the undergrowth is heavy and he stumbles. The traces gone. Look for memory in vain; try and forget and you can't. She was thin in the neck, Cone, and liked oranges. Liked to undress them. Slipped those slices in, let the juice run down. A transparent viper on her chin. Ben and I drove our vans in those days. St. Louis, Dallas sometimes. The road and the coffee warm in your palms and beer and snooker when the trips were finished and Ben your bones are chalk because of the trips I made alone. Is the boy dead who cut his initials there? Of course he is. A man now, all dead. The pup sleeps beneath my colored stones, and should I mourn him? Would he lie in vigil on my grave, or was he too much of a pup for such loyalty? Memory is the art of old men.

The other arts failed me. Hands too thick for leathercraft; watchbands I made resembled belts, belts resembled pulley straps, pulley straps resembled the steers from which it all began. Should've tried to take those leather scraps on the floor of the prison shop and build a cow. The art of tenderness escaped me, too. My infirmary, Cone, was a butcher shop. Didn't have the knack. Salt in their wounds. Joked when I should've wept, wept when I should've guffawed. Bedside manner poor. Stepped in bedpans. Watched the Mexican's swollen backside after they had whipped him and couldn't budge, couldn't lift an iodine bottle. The end of my hospital tour.

Father, Alice, Ben, the tamaracks of Time. The old man made and lost his money at stud, bunko, roulette, tiddledywinks, hopscotch. Would bet on the weather, on beans in a jar, on the speed of a cockroach, on the end of man. Liked Alice, too, because she gambled on her neck, her thighs, the shape of her cheek. Liked Ben for the chances he took running bootleg whiskey in the cold Chicago dawns, liked him for getting me to join him. And, at the last, liked me for the dare I took, for pulling the trigger. A ranch built of fantasy and ego. The outbuildings were never more than skeletons, but death repossessed a dream of elegance in the lodge: velvet chairs, walnut roundtables, ermine rugs. The airstrip: unfinished. The jazz bands: never summoned. The chandeliers: never lighted. Slow droplets from the mountain springs melt the rock and begin the avalanche; a continent slides into the Pacific, its frontier vanished, and the old man explains to me in the courtroom that violence was the natural thing, that Chicago is a violent city, that the age is violent. I see the cougar's leavings, the skin of a fawn, and believe him. My rocks are stained with the gore of indians, bison, antelope, wayward journeymen. My father, old gambler, was an American historian.

But the body of Alice comments on the centuries. What more can a silly man ask than beauty? What can a truckdriver dream? I imagined beauty as goodness, and that was my foolishness. The mountains, lovely killers, sit serene and cold. Alice, eroded by the boredom of her decoration, kissed me good-bye, kicked a tire on the van, and waved me off on my last route. Beauty: tolerate it, old storekeeper; have awe for it, but never worship it, never grow impassioned or jealous. Above the mountain our moon will soon burn like a fragrant wick, the stars will swim in harmony, the comets will mesmerize us. We are here, in this place,

*alive; in our sentence we learn our praise and pardon,
return to innocence, and fall in love with beauty once
again.*

Ossinger kicked a stone in the road and turned down
the last hill. His food box tapped his rump in rhythm
as he walked.

On the porch of the Polerbridge Store he kicked the
snow off his boots. Jenny, the collie bitch, greeted him
with quick, white puffs of her breath, and he watched
her carefully, studying her face for a trace of his dead
pup. Slowly, then, he opened the door and set his food
box beside the counter. An overpowering odor of hot
stew poured forth from Cone's rooms in the back; Ossinger's stomach tightened with noon hunger.

"Be with you in a minute!" Cone called. Then, when
his customer made no reply, he added: "Just go ahead
and take what you need!"

Ossinger stood in the middle of the room, rows of
canned goods towering around him. Crackers, apples,
yams, onions, candy, tobacco. He struggled with his
mackinaw, wrestled his hands free, and dropped it
across a stool beside the potbellied stove. His eyes
watered and he dabbed at them with his fist. Beyond,
through the opened door, he could see Cone's living
quarters, the shelves of books, the worn chairs, the pipe
rack and plastic humidor.

Silence hung in the room around him and he didn't
know what to do with himself. He listened to Cone
shuffle around the back room and breathed the deep,
meaty smell of the stew. He swallowed hard. His food
box glared at him from across the room, and he didn't
know whether to fill it or not. Beneath his unmoving
feet a small rivulet of melted snow appeared, and he
was slightly embarrassed for his presence, for his own

rank body odor, for his discourtesy to Cone on the road months ago.

Yet he walked over to the doorway and looked in. Cone stood, his back turned to Ossinger, stirring his meal. The silence grew until every bubble of the boiling stew seemed to pop distinctly in the room.

Ossinger looked up at the high shelves of books, swallowed hard again, and said, "You sure have a lot of books, Cone. Sure do."

Cone turned around suddenly. "Ossinger," he said. Drippings from the spoon which he held fell on his shoe, the floor, the edge of his cook stove. His brow knitted slightly; slowly, then, with a certain confusion of movement, he drew the spoon up to his lips, blew on it, and took a taste. "It's just right," he said. "Sit down and have some with me. It's the best I've ever made."

"Well," Ossinger said, taking the two steps to Cone's table, "I don't mind if I do."

Down the Blue Hole

This mystic arcadian village is called Poplar Bluff, Missouri, and, sure, you've heard of it, but you probably never knew that every day we have dozens of seances, prophecies by seers and visionaries, and the assorted practice of witches, astrologers, magicians, and even, perhaps, one ghoul.

This is the little town where I live, though I've thought of moving away because of all the competition. The pressure to exceed one's best effort is so awful here that I've considered moving up to St. Louis and losing myself in the mercenary and nonpsychic life.

For instance, the other night I had sixteen snickering tourists at my table, sitting in a circle with their hands extended and palms upright, lights out, and the thunder cracked and everybody jumped and screamed, their index fingers pricked so that a single drop of blood blossomed on each one. When I switched on the lights there they were, astounded—they all admitted it. And I blotted each finger with a Kleenex and put all the bloody tissues into my big glass cookie jar and told them wild stories about how I would mingle their blood and put them under a spell. They gasped and laughed and loved it. One of them asked how I ever did such a trick. Then they started talking about old Auntie Sybil, one of my competitors, and the whole effect dissolved.

Someone else wanted to know if I served refreshments.

My biggest act is my disappearing act where I just vanish. I go off into the Blue Hole, don't ask me how.

I've done this trick six times now: sit cross-legged under my velvet cloth, concentrate, melt my bones and my whole petty life into nothing, while the audience watches that cloth sag and empty itself. It's a great act because it's no act at all; off in the limbo of the Blue Hole I'm frightened, naturally, but I come back every time. Once I did this at the annual Rotary Banquet, vanishing under my velvet cloth at the rear of the hall, then coming up underneath the tablecloth beside the main speaker, rattling spoons and spilling ham loaf onto the floor, rising like Vesuvius forty feet from the spot where I disappeared. They were so pleased that they gave me an extra $25 and asked me back next year.

This is such a forlorn life for a great talent.

Funk and Wagnall's Encyclopedia describes our part of the state as flat and alluvial. Sort of dull, right: this is an agricultural stop, a market town for cotton and soybeans, a town with only a few important ranchers and a nice high school.

True, Mrs. Marybush, the town matron and benefactor, dresses like one of the key figures from the Tarot deck. Also, we have some housewives who give the evil eye to the butchers and the boys at the check-out counters at Krogers—where one can sometimes detect a slight levitation in the vegetable scale.

How this place happened I don't know. When I came

here years ago there were just a few spiritualists and a couple of horoscope addicts. I was just a country boy from over in Stoddard County, town of Zeta, and Poplar Bluff, I felt, had a ready audience for what I already reckoned was my considerable talent. Yet this town has become a kind of curse: tourists pour in all year, strangers all, there are loonies and charlatans everywhere, and the pressure, as I said, on one's craft is enormous.

Tourists are so unappreciative, too. One night I was making excellent contact with the dead at my table, summoning up a clear apparition, and this farmer recognizes the face and drawls, "Uncle Pardue, hey! This here is Bobby Wayne! Where'd you put that gold watch and fob you promised you'd leave me? We can't find that baby nowhere!"

Just as Las Vegas has its slot machines in the supermarkets, so our town exposes its soul in public; we have tea-leaf readers in every dumpy café, newsstands with astrological charts and no news, and one famous washerwoman—Auntie Sybil, yes—who advertises bona fide trances while she does up your clothes. In truth, Auntie Sybil's act is pretty good; she lives in a simple clapboard house on the edge of town, so a customer can drive out there with his bundle of wash and hear all the dire and wonderful predictions for his future while Auntie Sybil works. She's an old bag, about ninety, and very authentic. There with the Borax, her ironing board set up in her steamy kitchen, running your underwear through her old Maytag ringer, she communicates with the cosmos in your behalf. Also, voices from the past come straight out of her throat while she's in a trance— you pay $5 extra for this. She does a terrific Caesar Augustus and a good Mahatma Gandhi.

* * *

My name is Homer Bogardus, though after I left Stoddard County I dropped the first name altogether and my sign out front now reads Mr. Mystic, and, in smaller letters underneath, The Great Bogardus. This house of turrets, broad eaves and Gothic hallways is my castle and dismay—a pox, dammit, on the plumbing.

My memory of my early real world is dim and colorless, and, as I say about that, good riddance. Women, money, plumbing, friends: every reality I ever met addled and confounded me. The town of Zeta, symbolic in its very name of last things, almost ended me, true enough, and I used to contemplate mutilation and suicide in that cupboard of an upstairs room in Daddy's farmhouse. I might have been an idiot child chained to an iron bedstead and thrown crusts of bread, for it was that bad: I felt my adolescence like a disease, I pined, I bit my knuckles with anguish. One day—this was after hearing about Poplar Bluff and the lure of its underground—I fell into concentration and poured myself a glass of water from the pewter pitcher on the bureau although I sat twenty feet across my room in the window seat where I gazed out over Daddy's fields. I extended my physical powers across space and moved the pitcher and floated a brimming glass of water into my hands. Ninety magic days later I packed my bag and came in search of destiny.

Life before that, in all its lousy reality, was a wound. A strapping neighbor girl, Helen Rae, invited me into her barn, once, then successfully fought me off, breaking my collarbone in the fracas. My best buddy, Elroy, sabotaged my 4-H project for no reason at all. And Daddy died, to spite me for being different, I thought at the time—though in a seance, since, he materialized and denied it. And we were helplessly poor: cardboard innersoles in my dismal brogans.

So I left everything and hitchhiked to Poplar Bluff and the closets of my head.

What's so good about reality anyway? My bills are still mostly unpaid, my colleagues consider me odd in a town of oddities, my plumbing groans, my love life is asunder. Some days, like today, I dream beyond my powers—what if I *can* do almost anything?—to the Blue Hole where it might not be so bad to live forever.

"Produce a girl for me, a true love," I beg Auntie Sybil.

We're sitting in her famous kitchen while she makes lye soap. A Hollywood game show screams from her portable.

"You're unlucky in love," she offers.

"Don't give me that old line. I need what I need."

She fixes me with those depthless eyes; all mystery is behind those black slits, all knowledge, the dream of dreams. "All right, for fifty dollars cold cash I'll give it one hell of a try," she says.

"Conjure hard," I plead, peeling off the bills. "And for this price, please, I ought to get some fast action."

"You shouldn't even dally with the flesh, Bogardus," she tells me, putting my money under the radio. "You possess a great talent, enough for anyone to live for. If you had any talent for promotion, you could get on television."

That night a miracle enters my house. Sally Ritchie is a local girl back home from college, a strange, lovely spirit—incidentally thin of waist and ample of bosom—who has come, she says, in search of my netherworld. Her heart, she adds, has been broken by an athlete.

"Give me some sign," she breathes.

"I certainly will," I tell her, and I show her my collection of Oriental bells with no clappers. Then we sit holding hands in my parlor while I make them vibrate and ring.

"My god," Sally Ritchie breathes more heavily. "You are *good!*"

Though I'm trying to be in love and loved again, the town goes on as usual. In the church the minister begins his sermon and then begins to cry, as if possessed, a Black Mass.

Our postman, Mr. Denbo, refuses to deliver any more packages to the Cabal Institute because, he says, there are live things inside.

At the annual cakewalk some hippie warlocks and vampiresses appear, but Mayor Watson strolls across the gymnasium to reason with them.

"We don't want your kind here," he explains.

One of the kids gets sassy and gives the mayor some vulgar lip. "Decay," he says to the mayor. "Palsy. Extreme. Burp. Bloat. Pimple. Gronk. Kidney. Suck. Waddle."

Sally Ritchie contends that she adores me, but clearly she craves only the sensation of my powers; ever since I told her that I'm capable of complete dematerialization she has pleaded and insisted.

"Love me, not my talent," I ask of her, but she claims this is psychologically impossible. Her college boyfriend, the one who jilted her, played guard on the basketball team, she points out, and she adored his dribble.

She attends my nightly gatherings, applauding each wonder.

Tonight a dozen tourists receive a superior set of hallucinations: my old reptile-and-animal special. Encircling my table, hands touching, they sit and witness the ghostly albino Great Dane who moves through the room, passes into walls, emerges again. We detect his panting breath as he haunts us. This beast, I explain, and I tell them the absolute truth, has been a resident of this house for years, long before I came here; he is terribly restless. Harmless pet, no problem, I assure everyone, and they tilt first one way and then another—feel the pull of my fingers, Sally?—to glimpse him padding around.

Then the snakes: I move them into the room and have them slither across our shoes beneath the table. Hands tighten. Audible gasps. But this is just the frightening beginning; soon the serpents are coiling up and over us, a net of white underbellies over our arms and shoulders, and only my soothing voice prevents absolute hysteria.

The table is a writhing pit: black and green snakes everywhere. And now a thick furry adder: it rises among them like a sentinel, one large eye in the middle of its head, and I say, "Look at that eye, ladies and gentlemen, each one of you look into that eye!"

The one-eyed adder stops before each participant and stares him down. Meanwhile, the other serpents curl away and vanish—and the big one is gone, too, and the evening is a triumph.

"I could do my giant spider now," I tentatively offer.

"Oh, no, no, don't bother," everyone assures me.

"Wonderful," Sally Ritchie breathes. "And it was your eye in there, wasn't it, Mr. Bogardus? It was your eye inside that big snake, right?"

Deep in the Blue Hole.

I am here because Sally Ritchie wants a thrill.

The hole is like a cave, an indigo cavern, a gigantic drain which spirals down into the basements of the earth. Not so awful in here, really, after a time, so I sit here deciding exactly where I should now emerge. Should it be there in the parlor where I disappeared from Sally's side? No, I decide to make Sally suffer. I shall arise in the garden, calling and beckoning her outdoors so that she will find me bursting through the ground like a weird pod among all the dying autumnal stalks. A splendid gesture, true, so that's exactly how I do it: clods falling off my shoulders as I rise up, a primordial flower sprouting before her very eyes.

It occurs to me as I emerge that I'm trying to earn adoration.

"Forty minutes!" she breathes. "You were gone forty *minutes!* And look at you! Coming up through the *dirt!*"

"A new record," I observe. "Forty minutes in the Blue Hole."

The town ghoul, whose name is Ralph, is generally popular, but I find him morbid. He throws parties after which he tries to get Sally and her girl friends to stay late and go skipping around graveyards, but thank goodness they don't go for that sort of thing. I like Ralph well enough personally, but his art and mine are at odds; he tends to press reality home while I just want to divert and delight. Oh, I throw a few harmless scares into the tourists, sure, but why face them with war, pestilence, and man's cruel heart?

Ralph, like most people, can be somewhat deciphered by his rooms. I slip away from one of his cocktail parties at the Christmas season and tour his house, finding on the tables of his den and bedrooms stuffed hawks, daggers, a dusty crystal ball, and ashtrays made of old manacles. His bedroom is a gray, dim dungeon of a place.

A few days later, still thinking about rooms, I decide

to indulge in a little astral flight and visit my Sally's bedroom. She has the upstairs of her parents' big Georgian over on Maple Avenue.

I watch her sleeping, a brown shower of her lovely hair across the pillow.

Soon, I learn she is returning to school.

Do you want subtleties from me? The difference between my astral travels and complete dematerialization? All my mind-over-matter conquests explained? Do you want me to tell you why I'm so frivolous, why I don't use my powers to cure sickness, or, like that flashy French clairvoyant, fight crime and evil? Why should I compound my despair with endless explanation? What do you need except moments of profound awe?

Sally Ritchie writes that she is flunking biology.

It is darkest January and the Ozarks are blanketed in snow; at my window I can hear the world creaking beneath its ice, swaying and moaning in the winter thrall. The plumbing in my house answers noises.

I read my own palm and what do I see there? A private landscape as bleak as Poplar Bluff: a powerful life that can do all things, but is leaking away.

Accepting Ralph's invitation, I go over and catch the Super Bowl game on his crystal ball—nice reception, few ghosts, no commercials. We sit close at the table in his den, sipping cognacs, and staring into that small glass dream. Ralph, who is becoming morosely drunk, twitches his mustache and leers at me occasionally, but I don't mind.

"Thanks for asking me over," I tell him, and mean it.

In February I consider the Mardi Gras in New Orleans, the Acropolis, Kaanapali Beach in Hawaii, Marbella: all those vacation spots where I could go in an instant, where I could amaze the jet sets, charge supernatural fees, and forget Sally Ritchie and all the wretched consequences of my talents.

Instead, on the icy street outside the drugstore—valentine in hand, yes, ready for mailing—I draw my cape around me and tip my hat to Mrs. Marybush, who, today, is dressed like the Hanged Man. She smiles at my courtesy and informs me that she is sending friends from Kansas City to my table—skeptics, all, who need a good lesson.

"I'm not interested in the conversion of the masses," I snap at poor Mrs. Marybush. "Nor in offering proofs. Nor in metaphysical debate. I'm not going to call the lightning from the skies for another roomful of hicks. In fact, I'm retiring."

"No need to get huffy, Mr. Bogardus," she answers, and turns with her nose high and walks away.

In the spring there are county fairs, two of them, at Poplar Bluff and at Cape Girardeau more than fifty miles away, and I contract to perform my supreme act at them both—simultaneously.

The fair at Cape Girardeau is one of cheap tinsel and wheezing merry-go-rounds with all the splendor and illusion of a ghetto, yet the fairgrounds border the mighty Mississippi River, swollen with our winter rains, majestic, the elms and poplars on its banks rattling with extraordinary music.

All the people of my life mill around in the sunlit crowd: Daddy, Mr. Denbo, Auntie Sybil, Elroy, Mayor Watson, Helen Rae, Ralph, Mrs. Marybush, Sally Ritchie, and hundreds I haven't told you about.

Odors of mustard and cotton candy assail us. The television crew hurries around and the director, a sallow young man with a gold tooth, regards me with doubt—although the president of the Poplar Bluff Rotary Club has given assurances that this will absolutely come off as guaranteed. I eat a candied apple and gaze into the sky. A chilly day in April.

The cirrus clouds streak overhead, the pulse of the river is in us all, beating in our blood beneath the hurdy-gurdy sounds of the carnival; today I will melt away under my velvet canopy, I will enter the endless cavern of the Blue Hole, and rise again in Poplar Bluff, miles away, while two sets of cameras record the miracle.

A reporter from the *Post-Dispatch* interviews my colleagues, all of whom are here to bask in the fallout of publicity. There is Auntie Sybil, true to her down-home image, peddling a basket of lye soap and preserves among the crowd. That simple country crone. As Mrs. Marybush and the mayor sign up tourist business for the forthcoming seances, Ralph tells a reporter that "Poplar Bluff is the mysterious metaphor of America"— a phrase which the reporter scribbles in a small spiral notebook.

"You'll meet someone else," Sally Ritchie tells me as we lurk by a sideshow tent. "You have a lot to give."

Faced with Sally's clichés, I'm tempted to ask her to join me, to disappear with me this afternoon under the velvet—she's such a fool for all the hoopla and drumroll.

She wears an oversized letter sweater, oxfords, a ribbon in her hair. "I'll be proud," she goes on, "to say that I once knew you, Mr. Bogardus." She squeezes my hand, the only way she has ever touched me.

As I mount the stage, cameras whirring, the river glistening beyond the trees, a chilly breeze billowing up under my cape, I think of my house. Not too far away, there it stands: all boarded up at last, my sign removed, the furniture draped and covered in each room, chairs turned upside down on the great table where my powers ruled. I can visualize inevitable details: my kitchen faucet still dripping.

Will the Great Dane remain there, I wonder, to haunt the dust of those rooms? Will my absence be interpreted as failure or as just a mighty one-way effort into the unknown? Will this negate all the sad wonders of my life? Or will societies and scholars come to study me, to peruse my insurance policy and read the marginalia in my volumes? Will they seek to retrieve me in future seances? Or ask Sally Ritchie to recollect, to salvage memories and anecdotes?

The Cape Girardeau High School band plays "Columbia, the Gem of the Ocean," and down I go, I melt, going away, all gone, never to explain myself or my miracles again, not even these words that vanish now—poof!—upon this mysterious page.

Eating It

My first piece was a madeleine, one of those small French pastries and, yes, I ate it at my great-aunt's house. Auntie Drew had come down from Quebec to that sprawling, relic-filled lakeshore house in Wilmette north of Chicago. It was there I spent all the introspective summers of my youth—until my parents went down in a freak air crash—and then I moved in permanently, occupying the large, glassed-in porch and the east bedroom overlooking Lake Michigan all during the time I attended the University.

Auntie Drew's house had a smart Gallic kitchen: gleaming copper pans, knives at attention in a walnut rack, some delicious sauce always simmering on a rear burner. On the shelves of the reading room there were Proust's inevitable volumes and those of Balzac, Stendahl, Gide and others, but Auntie Drew's taste for French literature was mostly confined to those plain-wrapper jobs published by the Olympia Press. Pornography was her passion and she admitted it freely and, ah, how she loved those dirty little books with strumpets named Kitty or Daphne going down on gentlemen of the evening named Raoul or roughnecks named Skag, lots of kissing and licking and slurping. Her life was all saucy novels and novel sauces, if you'll excuse that, and she loved to cook for me and read me lurid passages while I sat at my desk working equations.

On a luxurious April afternoon filled with such interruptions (she had already ventured out onto the porch twice to read me succulent parts of her latest acquisition) she brought me that plate of French cookies.

The depth of Auntie Drew's sensualism might easily be miscalculated because, after all, she was a solid seventy years old and scrawny and blue all over: blue veins in her wrists, blue bags under her blue eyes, blue hair, and even a little blue tongue sloshing around in her mouth as she talked or ate with me. But a true sensualist she was—and an evangelist for the various pleasures of the skin. Finding that those tidbits from the Olympia Press just weren't exciting me, she brought out those cookies with a fierce determination.

By the time I had grabbed up three or four of them, though, she was hissing at me, "See here, Willie, roll the bite around in your mouth before you swallow! Just don't wolf them down like that! *Feel* the individual crumbs! The texture! Try to understand *taste!*"

Of course I didn't understand. The senses, taste included, were numb—for reasons I will struggle to convey to you later. But there we sat with that magnificent lake breeze filtering through a slightly opened glass panel, the porch all bright and wispy and full of April, the sun warming us, and I felt nothing; adrift in my usual cerebral cloud, I was cold as a machine and a madeleine was simply fuel, something to stoke my motor so that I could go down to the school to work equations for my dullard profs, so that I could polish my meager identity as a minor genius. My genius: ugh!

I'll tell you about that later, too, but first a bit more of that afternoon with Auntie Drew.

She became impatient with me.

"Now see here, you don't eat merely for the sake of your belly," she snapped at me. "You eat for the sake of your mouth or sometimes—with certain foods or beverages—for your throat's pleasure, but never, oh, please, Willie, slow down!"

Reaching across me, she turned the pages of my equations face down. "Take a deep breath," she urged me. "Just relax."

"To tell you the truth, Auntie, you make me a little nervous," I said, but obeyed orders.

"Of course you're slightly nervous, but things will come out all right," she assured me. "You're a perfectly normal boy, remember that. Just relax. Eating is an absolutely natural and relaxing activity, but sometimes one has to *learn* to be natural and relaxed. Just lean back."

Her smile—pale blue tongue and all—reassured me and she carefully guided the madeleine to my mouth, taking my slightly ink-stained fingers in her sweet and scrawny hand and moving it into place. Taking another deep breath, I made a real effort to concentrate on the flavor.

"Much better, Willie. Now you're getting it."

"You really think so?"

"Oh, yes, much better."

"I want it to be all right with you, Auntie."

"It's good for me, Willie, dear. Sure it's good for you?"

"It's very good for me."

In truth, as I munched I was getting slightly aroused to the spirit of it all. Detecting this, Auntie Drew pulled her chair closer to my desk and placed the dish at my elbow. Blue eyes glistened. A pause of our breath. From far off, a boat's horn on the lake.

"Now then," she said, "food isn't my particular way of life, but it might possibly be yours." She offered another madeleine. "Personally, I'm very visually oriented. I love the pictures I get in my mind's eye with all my dear books. And I love the flowers in my garden and the colors of the lake. Now I knew a gentleman in Capri once, Willie, who was very big on aphrodisiacs. Anything even remotely perfumed just scuttled him, and let me tell you, Willie, he liked some odd odors! Gunpowder, the sweatbands of hats, that sort of thing. Then there was your Cousin Orlie: you remember her? She was a real toucher, perhaps a touch*ee*, too, always patting and rubbing."

"These are really excellent cookies," I put in.

"Right, I believe you're catching on. Taste is your sensation."

"You notice I've slowed down?"

"Good, Willie, yes. But of course you should have savored your very *first* bite. If you want to experience true taste you can't do it after you're a dozen madeleines to the good."

A pause, please, in this central event of my life, this singular afternoon with Auntie Drew. If you imagine that you detect a murmur of disquiet, a tremor of abnormalcy in these doings, be put straight. I was, I am, I have always been a perfectly normal young man. I have had the juice of a thousand morning headlines in my time, have gone down for a few of the penny-arcade pleasures of lower State Street in this very city, and before my parents made their exit we traveled widely to all the fascinating places in Germany, Egypt,

Russia, and Harlem. I have done the things, as a child, that all children do: batted balls, run in competitions, dreamed nightmares, attended movies (Westerns and bloody technicolor epics), raised my voice to be heard, suffered a bully. I have visited indian burial mounds and circuses, football games and ice hockey. In my teens I had a girl who liked to drive out to the lakeside and talk metaphysics and sociology and another girl who liked to dance at the Fox River Bop Shop and who gave herself readily and often. I achieved musical recognition—don't we all want that?—by mastering the deep, steady rhythms of the portable electric organ (I was a chord man, yes) at that same Fox River establishment. My early grades were happily mediocre.

The truth is that all this somehow didn't move me. Or—just perhaps—moved me too much into numbness. But at any rate I found myself one day a collegiate cliché: alienated, aloof, silent, aimless, a bit blown out near the emotional fuse box. With deliberation and will I became an abstract intellectual, a mathematician, and the winters stretched out and enfolded me. When my wayfaring parents brushed a palm tree in their little Stinson and tipped over tipsyed and laughing into the sheen of the Ionian Sea, I shed no tear. Back in a cubicle at the school or out at my desk on the porch I simply worked another problem, felt a small satisfaction in its symmetry, and drew my identity around me like a cloak. Auntie Drew seemed a harmless eccentric, all nerve ends and giggles and nostalgia (she still lived in a world of speakeasies, bad gin, and the staggering madness of the Charleston, I imagined), so I ignored her. An illusion, yes, my small algebraic world, but a haven. At times I became mildly proud of my thinly disguised retreat into myself and my invulnerable crust; an assassination, a mugging down the block, the war.

Eating It

Auntie's giggle from a distant room, the polluted haze over the lake, nothing penetrated me.

You know, you do it yourself, this retreating. Done to perfection, we are each rewarded for it. We are called good citizens, sane, even geniuses.

But the days on the porch do arrive.

The madeleines do get eaten.

"Perhaps we should nibble on something else," I suggested to Auntie.

"That's the spirit," she said brightly, getting up. "Just remember, too, Willie, that *everything* is tasty." She said this with an intensity that made it seem profound.

"Everything deserves a bite? Is that the idea?"

"Exactly. That old wicker chair over there. Why don't you give it a chew?"

I got up with a shrug, approached it, and sank my teeth into its back.

"Well?" she asked, expectantly. "How is it?"

"Not too awfully edible," I said.

"Nonsense! Give it another try. And this time try to analyze its flavors! Try!"

"It's terribly tough."

"Just try, please!"

Concentrating, I consented to another bite. The flavors were, roughly, sixty-odd years of finely granulated dust, a slight hint of my deceased uncle's oily palms, a dash of the original greenwood fiber, and, unmistakably, a definite essence of nut bread. I related all this to Auntie Drew.

"You're coming along, Willie!" she said. "That's imaginative, too. Nut bread!"

My body was saying hello to itself and all its lost and forgotten parts; it was singing, all its juices and vitals in harmonious concert, and I followed my aunt into the living room.

Impulse took me and I broke off a piece of her Tiffany lampshade, a pretty green sliver of antique glass, and popped it right into my mouth. I thought she'd faint with happiness. "Oh, Will, oh my goodness," she swooned. Then: "How is it, dear? What's it got?" But before I could answer she smashed the whole lamp—expensive blue and green fragments everywhere—and grabbed up a bite for herself. A flash of her blue tongue.

"Glass is glass, I suppose, Auntie," I allowed. "But this seems like a pretty good piece of glass."

"It's a great piece of glass," she hissed. "Don't hold yourself back! Admit it!"

But the whole house waited to be devoured and I became distracted. The house was suddenly a forbidden fruit and I was inside it like a giddy parasite, eating out its core. Bites, bites, everywhere bites: I tasted the expensive velveteen drapes, the Italian love seat, the Persian rug (Kafir design), and the brocade pillows. Those pillows weren't too tasty—slick to the tongue, somewhat dry and stringy—but altogether substantial.

"I can't believe this of you, Will," Auntie Drew said with a whistle. "After all these months! This is so sudden!"

I smiled and nibbled a tassel on her French settee.

We reeled through the house now. In the kitchen, rejecting the obvious foodstuff in the refrigerator and cupboards, we chewed on a plastic bread box. "Take us!" cried the fern and ivy perched in the windowsill, so I gobbled them down. Magnificent greenery. After a plastic bread box my taste buds leapt with gratitude. "Suck me!" beckoned a stray French novel idling in the breakfast nook, so I held it under the water tap until it was dripping wet, then gave it a mighty suck. It was pasty, but deserved the gesture. "Nibble here!" cried the silk screen which hung in the sewing room, so I did.

Delirious, we circled back toward the porch, Auntie Drew in my wake, her hands dancing nervously in her blue hair and her laughter a dear and gentle spasm.

"You don't really mind this?" I asked breathlessly as I munched the pencils on my desk.

"A house is made to be eaten!" she hissed, grinning at me. "Never feel guilty for your abandon! Never!"

A line from one of her books, I said to myself, and I poked a nice eraser into my jaw. Yummy rubber.

"Your equations!" she said with inspiration. "Eat those!"

About here my senses began to blur.

Summoning all my willpower and saliva, I laughed and gagged and swallowed my past. The sunlight of the porch annointed us and Auntie—I followed her movements only vaguely—seemed to be devouring the television set off in the corner. A newscaster, full of grim modulations, was cut off in midsentence and I heard a crunch of tubes and the high crackle of his last breath. Adream, then, I followed into the yard where Auntie was twice her size, bulging and blue, and eating everything in sight except the trees and grass: the spears of the little iron fence bordering her yard, a minicar parked at the curb, a telephone pole. Then came a belch, sure as thunder, and Auntie, cracking her fingers to the distant strains of the Charleston, a large hungry flapper loosed on the population, was biting off smokestacks and high-rise apartment buildings and drinking Lake Michigan dry and feeding on the city. Hurriedly, I followed after her and popped the crumbs of her destruction into my mouth. Eat it all, we were saying in harmony, eat everything; choking, gagging, we stuffed it all in, and a happy nausea was overtaking me, a bliss of gluttony, the joy of the gorge.

The Pinball Machines

In those days the bottles stood at rigid amber attention on the shelves of my father's barbershop. The smells were bay rum, talcum, rose water, boot polish, and the cabbage odors of the Depression which sometimes filtered in from the streets.

Because my father supported three families—his sister and her family, my mother's brother and his—he kept long hours at the shop six days a week, hoping that someone might come in, climb into the chair, and order the works. Haircuts were 25¢, and 15¢ for children. Shaves were 15¢.

The only customer who ever ordered the works—haircut, shave, shampoo, and massage—was Mr. Robin. He was a fastidious man, always dusting the seat of the barber chair with his handkerchief, always pulling little sanitized tissues out of his pockets, always combing his hair two or three times after my father had finished with him. But he was rich. He owned the pinball machines that caused all the fuss. At first he wanted my father to put one into the shop, back beside the radiator, but my father said no. Then one evening as my

The Pinball Machines

father toweled off Mr. Robin's freshly shampooed hair, Mr. Robin said, "Look here, Red, I'm serious. You need a good pinball in here to brighten things up."

"My customers never have a spare nickel, Arnie," my father argued.

"Red, I'm counting on you to help me. That's the truth," Mr. Robin said. My father, knowing that he couldn't afford to lose such a good customer as Mr. Arnie Robin, consented. That first pinball machine entered our lives: standing back there in the corner like an obtrusive circus wagon, red with gold trim, with that old-fashioned slot in its belly where the nickels rolled out—assuming some lucky player ever hit JACKPOT and knocked over all the MAGIC SEVEN NUMBERS while scoring over nine hundred points. There were no flippers, no extra balls, not many fancy lights to run up the electricity bill like today's gaudy machines. For five cents a man got five balls and a sensitive TILT, and those steel balls dived into oblivion in a hurry.

Very early my father decided to answer my plea for a turn at the machine. "Okay, here's a nickel," he finally said. "Now in two minutes it'll be gone and you'll have nothing. Go ahead. See if it makes you feel any better to throw it down that slot." He took his position behind his chair and puffed on an Old Gold, content that life would soon teach me a lesson. I was thirteen years old and without shame, though, so I took my stance, popped that nickel in, and played my shots.

The nickels poured out. They filled the slot of the machine, fell onto my shoes, rolled noisily across the tile floor. My Uncle Edwin, who hung around the shop, Bertram, the young barber, and Jack the shine boy scampered around the spittoons with me and grabbed up the loot.

"Red!" my uncle finally yelled from the shine stand

where we counted my winnings. "Five dollars and twenty cents!" Everyone in the place winked and snickered. My father took a last draw on the butt of his cigarette and gazed out the shop window at the gathering twilight.

It was not always so silly and madcap, that life in 1935. The old man and woman who lived next door, Mr. and Mrs. Prine, stayed in bed all winter because the gas company had shut off their heat. My mother went from door to door with a laundry basket on her arm, asking for groceries for a young couple on the block who had four children and no supper. Our landlords twice asked us to move because we allowed too many aunts, uncles, and cousins to share our little apartments.

For amusement we sat on the porches in the neighborhood, told stories, and mustered some pretty good laughs. We sometimes walked to the zoo. On Sunday nights we went to the Astor Theater across from the barbershop: Adults, 10¢, Children, 5¢, Popcorn, 5¢. Cary Grant drank champagne, Irene Dunne and Greta Garbo drank champagne, and when Hedy Lamarr ran around naked in the forest I had to stay home with my cousins.

Sitting on those porches or walking home from the Astor or gazing into the familiar tired eyes of the giraffe at the Dallas Zoo during those years and months, I became awfully self-conscious. Large philosophic questions began to lay hold of me even then: who am I? what is the meaning of this time and place? what, oh, what does life mean?

My father, on the other hand, suffered none of this. He said little, and never anything remotely philosophic. His way was clear: you work or you go hungry. He was a man with things to do, and little to ponder.

Photographs—some in old rotogravure—of my father,

Red Baker, adorned the walls of the bathroom and hallway, photos taken in the 1920's when he had flair, when he wore striped shirts with garters on the sleeves, a jaunty bow tie, and sometimes carried a walking stick for no reason at all. He had left the farm in East Texas when he was fourteen to work as a busboy in a small Dallas hotel. When his family urged him to come back after a year to help with the cotton crop, he reluctantly obeyed. When the crop failed he started off again: Chicago, a year doing odd jobs, a short hitch in the army, another year working cotton, then his years playing poker. He was still gambling when he met my mother, fell under her Methodist spell, and married. Except for the striped shirts and gartered sleeves, he was completely converted. He went immediately to barber college and afterward bought the little shop in Oak Cliff. The Depression descended on us, but as I grew up I never thought of us as poor. Going off to the Astor on a rainy afternoon in 1933, I would have thought that everybody carried dry cardboard to slip into their shoes while they watched the movies.

My granny always stayed with us. When the railroad yards closed in Paducah, Kentucky, my Aunt Fay and Uncle Ben and my cousins joined us, too. The landlords began evicting us for overloading. In 1933 when the Red Cross called from Chicago to ask if we could accept my Uncle Edwin and his family, my folks had to say no. Uncle Edwin showed up anyway, though, slept on the couch, and walked every street in the city looking for work while his family stayed at a great-aunt's farm in North Texas. Uncle Ben, meanwhile, knocked door to door asking for household or yard chores.

My father, then, became the sole provider. He had a winning manner behind the barber chair and his customers always came ten at a time to murder his poor legs, to talk about that endless World Series, and to repeat the standard jokes. Unlike the barbers he hired, my father wouldn't hurry in order to get more customers. As a result he kept his customers longer, his reputation and business grew, and our livelihood stabilized. It is not unimportant that he was also a master barber, a craftsman. A man with no philosophy of life usually has an aesthetic. He used the electric clippers very little, spent long minutes aiming and snipping at single hairs, combing, standing back, taking aim again. Every head was a problem in the art.

"You know my customer, Mr. So-and-So," he'd say to me in those days.

"No, don't know who you mean," I'd usually say.

"The one who combs toward the front! Two parts in his hair! A little patch of gray over each ear!"

"I never pay attention to how anybody combs," I'd admit.

Work: that was the thing he knew. Perhaps this was why the pinball machine bothered him so much: it was a promise of something for nothing, a tease. My mother's Methodism, the Depression, all those mouths to feed hadn't made him completely grim and hapless with responsibility, but those photos in the bathroom and hallway of the old Red Baker were somehow tokens of the past.

Crisis lived with us, slept in our clothes, stalked us in the kitchen, hummed in our nerves as we sat on those easy porch swings, and strolled with us along those neighborhood streets where the windows opened like mouths on the night. We took a house on Eighth Street for eighteen dollars a month. Too much, but we had to have room. Uncle Edwin's family came down from the farm and took over the back bedroom and screened porch. Each week the government gave them an allotment of flour, corn meal, sugar, sowbelly, and lard—lovely inedible foodstuffs. My father, in turn, paid them cash for part of this so they could buy milk and meat.

Edwin became a problem. He grew surly and cynical. Concluding that there was no work to be found—he turned down a WPA job—he just stopped looking. "A little tobacco and corn bread, that's all I need," he kept saying. "To hell with knocking yourself out for such a life!"

He told my father that it was foolish to spend those early morning hours and late evening hours at the shop. "Keep your regular hours. Make your customers abide by them. If you're sitting in your shop at eleven at night, that's begging! You're a good barber, so don't beg!"

Edwin liked the pinball machine far too much. One afternoon he dropped sixty cents into it. Sixty cents.

"All right, Edwin, I hate to say this," my father told him that night, "but you're barred from the machine from now on."

"The hell you say," Edwin answered.

"All right, then, dammit, you're barred from the whole shop!"

Uncle Ben stepped between them. "Look," he said. "Let me eat this god-awful soup and corn bread in peace." Then he managed a laugh and everyone at the dinner table grinned weakly as Edwin and my father sat back down.

The next day when Edwin was in his usual chair at the shop chatting with the customers, my father came over and gave him a nickel. "Go hit the jackpot," he said. "There was an old sot in here this morning feeding nickels into the machine. It ought to be ready for a hit."

Concentrating hard, Edwin played his five balls and won six nickels. He left one of them on the cash register as he walked out.

Catastrophe appeared soon in the form of a nine-dollar grocery bill at a neighborhood market. We just couldn't pay it and a family conference on the matter produced only silence and hapless stares. Finally, my granny simply announced what all of us knew, but hesitated to say: "House rent is eighteen dollars a month. We just can't afford it. We'll have to find something smaller." Everyone groaned, but that was that. Mr. Hiller, the grocer, was informed that a plan was in operation. Of course it really wasn't. We knew there was nothing cheaper, nothing adequate for all of us.

A few evenings after that family conference I was helping Jack, our shine boy, sweep the shop when Mr. Robin came in. He gave me a candy cane. He patted the pinball machine. While my father finished a customer, Mr. Robin told two humorous stories which made all the men howl with laughter. Then before he stepped up into the chair he gave me his coat; the coat was heavy, pinstriped wool lined with blue silk and as I hung it on the peg I breathed its odors: good cigars, cologne, that deep wool smell. "The works," he told my father as he settled into the barber chair. His good mood infected us all.

Soon the other barbers and Jack were gone for the night and I was perched on the wire stool beside Mr. Robin and my father.

"I'm feelin' good," Mr. Robin announced, "because I've just bought sixteen new pinball machines. I'm gettin' rid of all those old models."

"That's mighty fine," my father said.

Silence. The thin noise of scissors. Mr. Robin sighed and turned to me. "Hear you're a big winner on that machine, son," he said.

"Five dollars and twenty cents," I answered, breaking into a grin.

"You're a lucky boy," Mr. Robin said. "What'd you do with the money?"

"Gave it to my mother," I said, still grinning.

Silence again. Mr. Robin gazed at himself in the mirror my father held and brushed a stray hair off his cheek. He didn't seem altogether happy with my last statement, and his eyes were hard and thoughtful. I watched the pile of Fitch lather atop his head and saw how my father bent him gently down into the lavatory and rinsed him off.

During the massage I watched Mr. Robin's face again. His eyes were closed in a pleasant euphoria. My father winked at me and together we enjoyed Mr. Robin's expressions. Afterward, as Mr. Robin stood before the big mirror combing himself—this always annoyed and partially insulted my father—I was allowed to brush him off with the little whisk broom. We then expected him to leave his usual small tip, empty the coins out of the pinball machine, say good night and depart, but he walked very slowly over to the shine stand and sat down. He had never done anything so familiar before. Also, the shine stand wasn't so clean and I worried about Mr. Robin's trousers.

"Red," he said slowly, "I want to give you my sixteen old pinball machines. There's probably two or three years left in them. I want you to have them outright. I can't trade them in for much, and they'll make you five or six dollars a week each."

My father swallowed hard.

"I'm goin' to offer you four locations, too," he went on. "Can't exactly make you my competitor, but I mean to help you. You'll have to work hard and get other locations for the machines on your own."

My father carefully put away his combs, removed his

smock, and opened the cash register to begin counting the day's receipts. He didn't answer.

"You want 'em?" Mr. Robin asked.

"Arnie," my father said, "I don't know."

"Don't know?"

That old poker player, I told myself. Old fox! We're rich, I wanted to shout. Rich!

"Can I let you know?" my father asked.

"Let me *know?*" Mr. Robin brushed imaginary talcum from his sleeve. The silence gathered again. "You're the best barber in town, Red," he finally said. "And we've known each other how long—six or seven years? And you think I haven't had my hair cut by those guys who come by appointment only? Sure I have! I had the guy from the Adolphus Hotel! But it's more than that, too. How much do you make a week?"

"Eighteen to twenty on a good week," my father answered.

This knowledge embarrassed me. So little? I tried to imagine the cost of Mr. Robin's pinstriped suit.

"Sixteen machines, Red, because I want to give 'em to you. And I want to do it. Get 'em all placed and you'll net five dollars a week easy on every one."

My father's temples pulsed and the color rose in his neck. "I just don't know," he said. "I can't decide."

Mr. Robin seemed disappointed that his offer hadn't ignited the room with enthusiasm.

"I'll have to let you know the next time you come in, Arnie," my father said. This was agreed on.

After Mr. Robin had gone I stood beside my father at the cash register.

"This machine doesn't make him more than two dollars a week," he said in an odd voice.

"But that's not the point," I squealed with excitement, no longer able to contain myself. "Free machines! We'll make money, *some* money!"

That night at dinner I blurted out Mr. Robin's offer before my father could make an announcement of it. He grew furious with me and sent me away from the table, but I listened from the bedroom as my uncles, Edwin especially, belittled my father's doubts.

"Isn't there any of that sweet wine left?" Edwin called, bounding around the kitchen, trying to celebrate. I hadn't heard him this enthusiastic in months. Uncle Ben sat at the table drawing up sets of figures. "Three hundred a month, at least!" he kept repeating. "Three hundred! Imagine!"

"I'm not sure yet, I tell you!" my father kept saying in reply.

"Ben and me'll take charge of 'em," Edwin offered, "so you can keep up your job at the shop, Red. We'll find little cafés for 'em. Places near factories where there'll be men with a little money. I know a spot down around the train depot. The postal employees go there. They always have some spare change."

As they talked long into the night, I grew sleepy and went into bed. Later in the dark house I heard my father's and my mother's voices. Fevered whispers. I lay awake wondering who I might become, struggling with the large and silly questions again, and wishing that I hadn't shot off my mouth and missed half my supper.

The following Sunday my father walked with me to the zoo. I knew this was a special walk, for my cousins weren't along, and I knew that my father was pondering the pinball machines, but he said nothing. We walked down into the large green valley where the Dallas Public Zoo hides in lush trees and elm-arched walkways. The lean animals stared out dolefully from their places: gaunt and indolent tigers, a dirty black bear, two sad elephants in a pit of old hay and manure. Years later I would come back to this place and there would be a fancy admission price, sleek cats, and puffy, fat birds. I would see no tattered fathers and sons strolling beneath those elms, no poor people anywhere, and I would distrust affluence and begin to understand my parents.

My father stopped and bought me an ice cream sandwich. Then we went down to the creek and he sat on a rock and pitched pebbles into a green pool beside some rocks for the remainder of the afternoon. Slowly, we strolled the two miles back to our neighborhood, but before we got home we stopped at the barbershop. For a few minutes I stood at the window watching the marquee of the Astor Theater. William Powell and Myrna Loy, I said to myself, I won't see you today. But then I began watching my father. In his solemn mood he stood before his multiple reflections in the shop mirrors, not really seeing himself at all, just seeing this place, his business, his work. His hand fell fondly on an old pair of scissors. The bottles gleamed around him: Lucky Tiger, Fitch, Wildroot, Bay Rum, Vaseline. The calendar on the wall offered his simple motto: It Pays To Look Well.

I suddenly knew that he'd never take those machines, and I knew, too, that his reasons would remain forever unutterable.

A few days later he told us his decision. My uncles couldn't believe it and when they finally did they were uncontrollable.

"Take the damned things and give them to me!" Edwin shouted at him. "Think of someone other than yourself, for Christsake!"

"How could I do that, Edwin?" my father argued. "Arnie Robin wants to do me a favor. How can I say, 'Give the machines to my brother-in-law'? I couldn't do it!"

"You selfish bastard!" Edwin shouted.

Uncle Ben was upset, too, and so were the ladies and so was I. No one understood.

"Pinball money isn't dirty money," Uncle Ben kept saying.

"That's right, Red," my mother put in, wanting to take everybody's side at once. "What's the matter with the machines? It wouldn't be like the old days—when you gambled with the food in our mouths. And it's how we *use* the money that counts!"

"The truth is," my granny said, "that Red just doesn't want those machines—because they just aren't his kind of thing. Right?"

"Right!" my father said.

That stopped the argument for a moment. No one knew what to say or how.

"He's a barber," my granny explained to everyone.

"That's right," my father said.

"What in *hell* is that supposed to mean?" Edwin persisted.

"A man has his work and that's that," I suddenly added. Mother and Aunt Fay quickly told me to keep my mouth shut.

I wasn't in the shop a few days later when my father told Mr. Robin that he couldn't accept the machines, and when he asked Mr. Robin, who owned several houses in that part of town, if he could possibly help find us a new place to live instead.

When we moved into the new house, Edwin took his family back to the farm in North Texas.

The new house—which my father bought for very

small monthly payments—stood next to a vacant lot which was also owned by Mr. Robin and we had permission to turn that open field into a garden. We bought chicken wire, went down to McDonald's Hatchery and bought baby chicks, and started that miraculous garden which saved us. Onions, beets, green beans, limas, peas, okra, and tomatoes sprouted everywhere, and I became proud with my Uncle Ben, Aunt Fay, and mother that our hands soon grew so rough and hard with the work we did outdoors. At night we put our hands on the kitchen table, my father and I, and mine were brown and rough and his were pink and soft from his work around the barbershop lavatories.

Soon my Uncle Ben was called back to the railroad yards in Kentucky. Our house received three bright coats of white paint. My granny died. The luck which had once spilled five dollars and twenty cents onto my shoes stayed with me through Europe during the war.

I have been a dreamer all my days, one who speaks too much about values and moralities, one who has too much philosophy, too many silly questions about the nature of things. Meanwhile my father, Red Baker, opens and closes the door of his barbershop, offers his service, and in the late evening strolls down Bishop Avenue toward home in the knowledge that he has paid the mortgage on his era.

Roller Ball Murder

The game, the game: here we go again. All glory to it, all things I am and own because of Roller Ball Murder.

Our team stands in a row, twenty of us in salute as the corporation hymn is played by the band. We view the hardwood oval track which offers us the bumps and rewards of mayhem: fifty yards long, thirty yards across the ends, high banked, and at the top of the walls the cannons which fire those frenzied twenty-pound balls—similar to bowling balls, made of ebonite—at velocities over three hundred miles an hour. The balls careen around the track, eventually slowing and falling with diminishing centrifugal force, and as they go to ground or strike a player another volley fires. Here we are, our team: ten roller skaters, five motorbike riders, five runners (or clubbers). As the hymn plays, we stand erect and tough; eighty thousand sit watching in the stands and another two billion viewers around the world inspect the set of our jaws on multivision.

The runners, those bastards, slip into their heavy leather gloves and shoulder their lacrosselike paddles—with which they either catch the whizzing balls or bash the rest of us. The bikers ride high on the walls (beware, mates, that's where the cannon shots are too hot to handle) and swoop down to help the runners at opportune times. The skaters, those of us with the juice for it, protest: we clog the way, try to keep the runners from passing us and scoring points, and become the fodder in the brawl. So two teams of us, forty in all, go skating and running and biking around the track while the big balls are fired in the same direction as we move —always coming up behind us to scatter and maim us— and the object of the game, fans, as if you didn't know, is for the runners to pass all skaters on the opposing team, field a ball, and pass it to a biker for one point. Those bikers, by the way, may give the runners a lift— in which case those of us on skates have our hands full overturning 175cc motorbikes.

No rest periods, no substitute players. If you lose a man, your team plays short.

Today I turn my best side to the cameras. I'm Jonathan E, none other, and nobody passes me on the track. I'm the core of the Houston team and for the two hours of play—no rules, no penalties once the first cannon fires—I'll level any bastard runner who raises a paddle at me.

We move: immediately there are pileups of bikes, skaters, referees, and runners, all tangled and punching and scrambling when one of the balls zooms around the corner and belts us. I pick up momentum and heave an opposing skater into the infield at center ring; I'm brute speed today, driving, pushing up on the track, dodging a ball, hurtling downward beyond those bastard runners. Two runners do hand-to-hand combat and one gets his helmet knocked off in a blow which tears away half his face; the victor stands there too long admiring his work and gets wiped out by a biker who swoops down and flattens him. The crowd screams and I know the cameramen have it on an isolated shot and that viewers in Melbourne, Berlin, Rio, and L.A. are heaving with excitement in their easy chairs.

When an hour is gone I'm still wheeling along, naturally, though we have four team members out with broken parts, one rookie maybe dead, two bikes demolished. The other team, good old London, is worse off.

One of their motorbikes roars out of control, takes a hit from one of the balls, and bursts into flame. Wild cheering.

Cruising up next to their famous Jackie Magee, I time my punch. He turns in my direction, exposes the ugly snarl inside his helmet, and I take him out of action. In that tiniest instant, I feel his teeth and bone give way and the crowd screams approval. We have them now, we really have them, we do, and the score ends 7—2.

The years pass and the rules alter—always in favor of a greater crowd-pleasing carnage. I've been at this more than fifteen years, amazing, with only broken arms and collarbones to slow me down, and I'm not as spry as ever, but meaner—and no rookie, no matter how much in shape, can learn this slaughter unless he comes out and takes me on in the real thing.

But the rules. I hear of games in Manila, now, or in Barcelona with no time limits, men bashing each other until there are no more runners left, no way of scoring points. That's the coming thing. I hear of Roller Ball Murder played with mixed teams, men and women, wearing tear-away jerseys which add a little tit and vulnerable exposure to the action. Everything will happen. They'll change the rules until we skate on a slick of blood, we all know that.

Before this century began, before the Great Asian war of the 1990's, before the corporations replaced nationalism and the corporate police forces supplanted the world's armies, in the last days of American football and the World Cup in Europe, I was a tough young rookie who knew all the rewards of this game. Women: I had them all—even, pity, a good marriage once. I had so much money after my first trophies that I could buy houses and land and lakes beyond the huge cities where only the executive class was allowed. My photo, then, as now, was on the covers of magazines, so that my name and the name of the sport were one, and I was Jonathan E, no other, a survivor and much more in the bloodiest sport.

At the beginning I played for Oil Conglomerates, then those corporations became known as ENERGY; I've always played for the team here in Houston, they've given me everything.

"How're you feeling?" Mr. Bartholemew asks me. He's taking the head of ENERGY, one of the most powerful men in the world, and he talks to me like I'm his son.

"Feeling mean," I answer, so that he smiles.

He tells me they want to do a special on multivision about my career, lots of shots on the side screens showing my greatest plays, and the story of my life, how ENERGY takes in such orphans, gives them work and protection, and makes careers possible.

"Really feel mean, eh?" Mr. Bartholemew asks again, and I answer the same, not telling him all that's inside me because he would possibly misunderstand; not telling him that I'm tired of the long season, that I'm lonely and miss my wife, that I yearn for high, lost, important thoughts, and that maybe, just maybe, I've got a deep rupture in the soul.

An old buddy, Jim Cletus, comes by the ranch for the weekend. Mackie, my present girl, takes our dinners out of the freezer and turns the rays on them; not so domestic, that Mackie, but she has enormous breasts and a waist smaller than my thigh.

Cletus works as a judge now. At every game there are two referees—clowns, whose job it is to see nothing amiss—and the judge who records the points scored. Cletus is also on the International Rules Committee and tells me they are still considering several changes.

"A penalty for being lapped by your own team, for one thing," he tells us. "A damned simple penalty, too: they'll take off your helmet."

Mackie, bless her bosom, makes an O with her lips.

Cletus, once a runner for Toronto, fills up my oversized furniture and rests his hands on his bad knees.

"What else?" I ask him. "Or can you tell me?"

"Oh, just financial things. More bonuses for superior attacks. Bigger bonuses for being named World All-Star —which ought to be good news for you again. And, yeah, talk of reducing the two-month off-season. The viewers want more."

After dinner Cletus walks around the ranch with me. We trudge up the path of a hillside and the Texas countryside stretches before us. Pavilions of clouds.

"Did you ever think about death in your playing days?" I ask, knowing I'm a bit too pensive for old Clete.

"Never in the game itself," he answers proudly. "Off the track—yeah, sometimes I never thought about anything else."

We pause and take a good long look at the horizon.

"There's another thing going in the Rules Committee," he finally admits. "They're considering dropping the time limit—at least, god help us, Johnny, the suggestion has come up officially."

I like a place with rolling hills. Another of my houses is near Lyons in France, the hills similar to these although more lush, and I take my evening strolls there over an ancient battleground. The cities are too much, so large and uninhabitable that one has to have a business passport to enter such immensities as New York.

"Naturally I'm holding out for the time limit," Cletus goes on. "I've played, so I know a man's limits. Sometimes in that committee, Johnny, I feel like I'm the last moral man on earth sitting there and insisting that there should be a few rules."

The statistical nuances of Roller Ball Murder entertain the multitudes as much as any other aspect of the game. The greatest number of points scored in a single game: 81. The highest velocity of a ball when actually caught by a runner: 176 mph. Highest number of players put out of action in a single game by a single skater: 13—world's record by yours truly. Most deaths in a single contest: 9—Rome vs. Chicago, December 4, 2012.

The giant lighted boards circling above the track monitor our pace, record each separate fact of the slaughter, and we have millions of fans—strange, it always seemed to me—who never look directly at the action, but just study those statistics.

A multivision survey established this.

Before going to the stadium in Paris for our evening game, I stroll under the archways and along the Seine. Some of the French fans call to me, waving and talking to my bodyguards as well, so I become oddly conscious of myself, conscious of my size and clothes and the way I walk. A curious moment.

I'm six-foot three inches and weigh 255 pounds. My neck is 18½ inches. Fingers like a pianist. I wear my conservative pinstriped jump suit and the famous flat Spanish hat. I am 34 years old now, and when I grow old, I think, I'll look a lot like the poet Robert Graves.

The most powerful men in the world are the executives. They run the major corporations which fix prices, wages, and the general economy, and we all know they're crooked, that they have almost unlimited power and money, but I have considerable power and money myself and I'm still anxious. What can I possibly want, I ask myself, except, possibly, more knowledge?

I consider recent history—which is virtually all anyone remembers—and how the corporate wars ended, so that we settled into the Six Majors: ENERGY, TRANSPORT, FOOD, HOUSING, SERVICES, and LUXURY. Sometimes I forget who runs what—for instance, now that the universities are operated by the Majors (and provide the farm system for Roller Ball Murder), which Major runs them? SERVICES or LUXURY? Music is one of our biggest industries, but I can't remember who administers it. Narcotic research is now under FOOD, I know, though it used to be under LUXURY.

Anyway, I think I'll ask Mr. Bartholemew about knowledge. He's a man with a big view of the world, with values, with memory. My team flings itself into the void while his team harnesses the sun, taps the sea, finds new alloys, and is clearly just a hell of a lot more serious.

* * *

The Mexico City game has a new wrinkle: they've changed the shape of the ball on us.

Cletus didn't even warn me—perhaps he couldn't—but here we are playing with a ball not quite round, its center of gravity altered, so that it rumbles around the track in irregular patterns.

This particular game is bad enough because the bikers down here are getting wise to me; for years, since my reputation was established, bikers have always tried to take me out of a game early. But early in the game I'm wary and strong and I'll always gladly take on a biker—even since they put shields on the motorbikes so that we can't grab the handlebars. Now, though, these bastards know I'm getting older—still mean, but slowing down, as the sports pages say about me—so they let me bash it out with the skaters and runners for as long as possible before sending the bikers after me. Knock out Jonathan E, they say, and you've beaten Houston; and that's right enough, but they haven't done it yet.

The fans down here, all low-class FOOD workers mostly, boil over as I manage to keep my cool—and the oblong ball, zigzagging around at lurching speeds, hopping two feet off the track at times, knocks out virtually their whole team. Finally, some of us catch their last runner/clubber and beat him to a pulp, so that's it: no runners, no points. Those dumb FOOD workers file out of the stadium while we show off and score a few fancy and uncontested points. The score 37—4. I feel wonderful, like pure brute speed.

Mackie is gone—her mouth no longer makes an O around my villa or ranch—and in her place is the new one, Daphne. My Daphne is tall and English and likes photos—always wants to pose for me. Sometimes we get out our boxes of old pictures (mine as a player, mostly, and hers as a model) and look at ourselves, and it occurs to me that the photos spread out on the rug are the real us, our public and performing true selves, and the two of us here in the sitting room, Gaelic gray winter outside our window, aren't too real at all.

"Look at the muscles in your back!" Daphne says in amazement as she studies a shot of me at the California beach—and it's as though she never before noticed.

After the photos, I stroll out beyond the garden. The brown waving grass of the fields reminds me of Ella, my only wife, and of her soft long hair which made a tent over my face when we kissed.

I lecture to the ENERGY-sponsored rookie camp and tell them they can't possibly comprehend anything until they're out on the track getting belted.

My talk tonight concerns how to stop a biker who wants to run you down. "You can throw a shoulder right into the shield," I begin. "And that way it's you or him."

The rookies look at me as though I'm crazy.

"Or you can hit the deck, cover yourself, tense up, and let the bastard flip over your body," I go on, counting on my fingers for them and doing my best not to laugh. "Or you can feint, sidestep up hill, and kick him off the track—which takes some practice and timing."

None of them knows what to say. We're sitting in the infield grass, the track lighted, the stands empty, and their faces are filled with stupid awe. "Or if a biker comes at you with good speed and balance," I continue, "then naturally let the bastard by—even if he carries a runner. That runner, remember, has to dismount and field one of the new odd-shaped balls which isn't easy—and you can usually catch up."

The rookies begin to get a smug look on their faces

when a biker bears down on me in the demonstration period.

Brute speed. I jump to one side, dodge the shield, grab the bastard's arm and separate him from his machine in one movement. The bike skids away. The poor biker's shoulder is out of socket.

"Oh yeah," I say, getting back to my feet. "I forgot about that move."

Toward midseason when I see Mr. Bartholemew again he has been deposed as the chief executive at ENERGY. He is still very important, but lacks some of the old certainty; his mood is reflective, so that I decide to take this opportunity to talk about what's bothering me.

We lunch in Houston Tower, viewing an expanse of city. A nice Beef Wellington and Burgundy. Daphne sits there like a stone, probably imagining that she's in a movie.

"Knowledge, ah, I see," Mr. Bartholemew replies in response to my topic. "What're you interested in, Jonathan? History? The arts?"

"Can I be personal with you?"

This makes him slightly uncomfortable. "Sure, naturally," he answers easily, and although Mr. Bartholemew isn't especially one to inspire confession I decide to blunder along.

"I began in the university," I remind him. "That was —let's see—more than seventeen years ago. In those days we still had books and I read some, quite a few, because I thought I might make an executive."

"Jonathan, believe me, I can guess what you're going to say," Mr. Bartholemew sighs, sipping the Burgundy and glancing at Daphne. "I'm one of the few with real regrets about what happened to the books. Everything is still on tapes, but it just isn't the same, is it? Nowadays only the computer specialists read the tapes and we're right back in the Middle Ages when only the monks could read the Latin script."

"Exactly," I answer, letting my beef go cold.

"Would you like me to assign you a specialist?"

"No, that's not exactly it."

"We have the great film libraries: you could get a permit to see anything you want. The Renaissance. Greek philosophers. I saw a nice summary film on the life and thought of Plato once."

"All I know," I say with hesitation, "is Roller Ball Murder."

"You don't want out of the game?" he asks warily.

"No, not at all. It's just that I want—god, Mr. Bartholemew, I don't know how to say it: I want *more*."

He offers a blank look.

"But not things in the world," I add. "More for *me*."

He heaves a great sigh, leans back, and allows the steward to refill his glass. Curiously, I know that he understands; he is a man of sixty, enormously wealthy, powerful in our most powerful executive class, and behind his eyes is the deep, weary, undeniable comprehension of the life he has lived.

"Knowledge," he tells me, "either converts to power or it converts to melancholy. Which could you possibly want, Jonathan? You *have* power. You have status and skill and the whole masculine dream many of us would like to have. And in Roller Ball Murder there's no room for melancholy, is there? In the game the mind exists for the body, to make a harmony of havoc, right? Do you want to change that? Do you want the mind to exist for itself alone? I don't think you actually want that, do you?"

"I really don't know," I admit.

"I'll get you some permits, Jonathan. You can see video films, learn something about reading tapes, if you want."

"I don't think I really *have* any power," I say, still groping.

"Oh, come on. What do *you* say about that?" he asks, turning to Daphne.

"He definitely has power," she answers with a wan smile.

Somehow the conversation drifts away from me; Daphne, on cue, like the good spy for the corporation she probably is, begins feeding Mr. Bartholemew lines and soon, oddly enough, we're discussing my upcoming game with Stockholm.

A hollow space begins to grow inside me, as though fire is eating out a hole. The conversation concerns the end of the season, the All-Star Game, records being set this year, but my disappointment—in what, exactly, I don't even know—begins to sicken me.

Mr. Bartholemew eventually asks what's wrong.

"The food," I answer. "Usually I have great digestion, but maybe not today."

In the locker room the dreary late-season pall takes us. We hardly speak among ourselves, now, and like soldiers or gladiators sensing what lies ahead, we move around in these sickening surgical odors of the locker room.

Our last training and instruction this year concerns the delivery of deathblows to opposing players; no time now for the tolerant shoving and bumping of yesteryear. I consider that I possess two good weapons: because of my unusually good balance on skates, I can often shatter my opponent's knee with a kick; also, I have a good backhand blow to the ribs and heart, if, wheeling along side by side with some bastard, he raises an arm against me. If the new rules change removes a player's helmet, of course, that's death; as it is right now (there are rumors, rumors every day about what new version of RBM we'll have next) you go for the windpipe, the ribs or heart, the diaphragm, or anyplace you don't break your hand.

Our instructors are a pair of giddy Oriental gentlemen who have all sorts of anatomical solutions for us and show drawings of the human figure with nerve centers painted in pink.

"What you do is this," says Moonpie, in parody of these two. Moonpie is a fine skater in his fourth season and fancies himself an old-fashioned drawling Texan. "What you do is hit 'em on the jawbone and drive it up into their ganglia."

"Their *what*?" I ask, giving Moonpie a grin.

"Their goddamned *ganglia*. Bunch of nerves right here underneath the ear. Drive their jawbones into that mess of nerves and it'll ring their bells sure."

Daphne is gone now, too, and in this interim before another companion arrives, courtesy of all my friends and employers at ENERGY, Ella floats back into my dreams and daylight fantasies.

I was a corporation child, some executive's bastard boy, I always preferred to think, brought up in the Galveston section of the city. A big kid, naturally, athletic and strong—and this, according to my theory, gave me healthy mental genes, too, because I take it now that strong in body is strong in mind: a man with brute speed surely also has the capacity to mull over his life. Anyway, I married at age fifteen while I worked on the docks for Oil Conglomerates. Ella was a secretary, slim with long brown hair, and we managed to get permits to both marry and enter the university together. Her fellowship was in General Electronics—she was clever, give her that—and mine was in Roller Ball Murder. She fed me well that first year, so I put on thirty hard pounds and at night she soothed my bruises (was she a spy, too, I've sometimes wondered, whose job it was to prime the bull for the charge?) and perhaps it was because she was my first woman ever, eighteen years old, lovely, that I've never properly forgotten.

She left me for an executive, just packed up and went to Europe with him. Six years ago I saw them at a sports banquet where I was presented an award: there they were, smiling and being nice, and I asked them only one question, just one, "You two ever had children?" It gave me odd satisfaction that they had applied for a permit, but had been denied.

Ella, love: one does consider: did you beef me up and break my heart in some great design of corporate society?

There I was, whatever, angry and hurt. Beyond repair, I thought at the time. And the hand which stroked Ella soon dropped all the foes of Houston.

I take sad stock of myself in this quiet period before another woman arrives; I'm smart enough, I know that: I had to be to survive. Yet, I seem to know nothing—and can feel the hollow spaces in my own heart. Like one of those computer specialists, I have my own brutal technical know-how; I know what today means, what tomorrow likely holds, but maybe it's because the books are gone—Mr. Bartholemew was right, it's a shame they're transformed—that I feel so vacant. If I didn't remember my Ella—this I realize—I wouldn't even *want* to remember because it's love I'm recollecting as well as those old university days.

Recollect, sure: I read quite a few books that year with Ella and afterward, too, before turning professional in the game. Apart from all the volumes about how to get along in business, I read the history of the kings of England, that pillars of wisdom book by T. E. Lawrence, all the forlorn novels, some Rousseau, a bio of Thomas Jefferson, and other odd bits. On tapes now, all that, whirring away in a cool basement someplace.

The rules crumble once more.

At the Tokyo game, we discover that there will be three oblong balls in play at all times.

Some of our most experienced players are afraid to go out on the track. Then, after they're coaxed and threatened and finally consent to join the flow, they fake injury whenever they can and sprawl in the infield like rabbits. As for me, I play with greater abandon than ever and give the crowd its money's worth. The Tokyo skaters are either peering over their shoulders looking for approaching balls when I smash them, or, poor devils, they're looking for me when a ball takes them out of action.

One little bastard with a broken back flaps around for a moment like a fish, then shudders and dies.

Balls jump at us as though they have brains.

But fate carries me, as I somehow know it will; I'm a force field, a destroyer. I kick a biker into the path of a ball going at least two hundred miles an hour. I swerve around a pileup of bikes and skaters, ride high on the track, zoom down, and find a runner/clubber who panics and misses with a roundhouse swing of his paddle; without much ado, I belt him out of play with the almost certain knowledge—I've felt it before—that he's dead before he hits the infield.

One ball flips out of play soon after being fired from the cannon, jumps the railing, sails high, and plows into the spectators. Beautiful.

I take a hit from a ball, one of the three or four times I've ever been belted. The ball is riding low on the track when it catches me and I sprawl like a baby. One bastard runner comes after me, but one of our bikers chases him off. Then one of their skaters glides by and takes a shot at me, but I dig him in the groin and discourage him, too.

Down and hurting, I see Moonpie killed. They take off his helmet, working slowly—it's like slow motion and I'm writhing and cursing and unable to help—and open his mouth on the toe of some bastard skater's boot. Then they kick the back of his head and knock out all his teeth—which rattle downhill on the track. Then kick again and stomp: his brains this time. He drawls a last groaning good-bye while the cameras record it.

And later I'm up, pushing along once more, feeling bad, but knowing everyone else feels the same; I have that last surge of energy, the one I always get when I'm going good, and near the closing gun I manage a nice move: grabbing one of their runners with a headlock, I skate him off to limbo, bashing his face with my free fist, picking up speed until he drags behind like a dropped flag, and disposing of him in front of a ball which carries him off in a comic flop. Oh, god, god.

Before the All-Star Game, Cletus comes to me with the news I expect: this one will be a no-time-limit extravaganza in New York, every multivision set in the world tuned in. The bikes will be more high-powered, four oblong balls will be in play simultaneously, and the referees will blow the whistle on any sluggish player and remove his helmet as a penalty.

Cletus is apologetic.

"With those rules, no worry," I tell him. "It'll go no more than an hour and we'll all be dead."

We're at the Houston ranch on a Saturday afternoon, riding around in my electrocart viewing the Santa Gertrudis stock. This is probably the ultimate spectacle of my wealth: my own beef cattle in a day when only a few special members of the executive class have any meat to eat with the exception of mass-produced fish. Cletus is so impressed with my cattle that he keeps going on this afternoon and seems so pathetic to me, a judge who doesn't judge, the pawn of a committee, another feeble hulk of an old RBM player.

"You owe me a favor, Clete," I tell him.

"Anything," he answers, not looking me in the eyes.

I turn the cart up a lane beside my rustic rail fence, an archway of oak trees overhead and the early spring bluebonnets and daffodils sending up fragrances from the nearby fields. Far back in my thoughts is the awareness that I can't possibly last and that I'd like to be buried out here—burial is seldom allowed anymore, everyone just incinerated and scattered—to become the mulch of flowers.

"I want you to bring Ella to me," I tell him. "After all these years, yeah: that's what I want. You arrange it and don't give me any excuses, okay?"

We meet at the villa near Lyons in early June, only a week before the All-Star Game in New York, and I think she immediately reads something in my eyes which helps her to love me again. Of course I love her: I realize, seeing her, that I have only a vague recollection of being alive at all, and that was a long time ago, in another century of the heart when I had no identity except my name, when I was a simple dock worker, before I ever saw all the world's places or moved in the rumbling nightmares of Roller Ball Murder.

She kisses my fingers. "Oh," she says softly, and her face is filled with true wonder, "what's happened to you, Johnny?"

A few soft days. When our bodies aren't entwined in lovemaking, we try to remember and tell each other everything: the way we used to hold hands, how we fretted about receiving a marriage permit, how the books looked on our shelves in the old apartment in River Oaks. We strain, at times, trying to recollect the impossible; it's true that history is really gone, that we have no families or touchstones, that our short personal lives alone judge us, and I want to hear about her husband, the places they've lived, the furniture in her house, anything. I tell her, in turn, about all the women, about Mr. Bartholemew and Jim Cletus, about the ranch in the hills outside Houston.

Come to me, Ella. If I can remember us, I can recollect meaning and time.

It would be nice, I think, once, to imagine that she was taken away from me by some malevolent force in this awful age, but I know the truth of that: she went away, simply, because I wasn't enough back then, because those were the days before I yearned for anything, when I was beginning to live to play the game. But no matter. For a few days she sits on my bed and I touch her skin like a blind man groping back over the years.

On our last morning together she comes out in her traveling suit with her hair pulled up underneath a fur cap. The softness has faded from her voice and she smiles with efficiency, as if she has just come back to the practical world; I recall, briefly, this scene played out a thousand years ago when she explained that she was going away with her executive.

She plays like a biker, I decide; she rides up there high above the turmoil, decides when to swoop down, and makes a clean kill.

"Good-bye, Ella," I say, and she turns her head slightly away from my kiss so that I touch her fur cap with my lips.

"I'm glad I came," she says politely. "Good luck, Johnny."

New York is frenzied with what is about to happen.

The crowds throng into Energy Plaza, swarm the ticket offices at the stadium, and wherever I go people are reaching for my hands, pushing my bodyguards away, trying to touch my sleeve as though I'm some ancient religious figure, a seer or prophet.

Before the game begins I stand with my team as the corporation hymns are played. I'm brute speed today, I tell myself, trying to rev myself up; yet, adream in my thoughts, I'm a bit unconvinced.

A chorus of voices joins the band now as the music swells.

The game, the game, all glory to it, the music rings, and I can feel my lips move with the words, singing.

The Blurb King

"One of the great stories!"
—H. Neal

"Watch Harrison, that trickster!"
—T. S. Eliot

My name is Harry Neal, the Blurb King, although at times I've used other forms and signatures according to what I've blurbed, and I've programmed my computer to tell you this success story—which is really yours as well as mine.

In my time I've been a boy athlete, salesman, executive, and minor poet, but all this came before I got into the blurb business—which is the vocation of endorsement and promotion by way of giving away your name. Attach, please, no deep psychological significance to this activity. One can give away one's name an endless number of times and yet always keep it; it isn't remotely degrading, as some claim, and the rewards of blurbing are many, as you will see.

Blurbing is related to the art of critical appraisal, but only indirectly since it is a more concise form and really just lays out a quick opinion. Nobody wants to suffer a long critique nowadays, after all, which begins with definitions of terms and runs through historical survey and culminates in intellectual analysis and perspective. Can you imagine my old high-school football coach in conference with his brutish assistants back there in Three Rivers, Texas, and he says, "Okay, has Neal got it at linebacker or not?" and one of them gives him a discussion of Spartan youth, the nature of American linebacking since Rockne, and a neo-Freudian overview of my life-style? No, one of them has to snap, "Lots of guts, that kid! He'll do a job for us!" and that's a blurb, one of the first blurbs of my life, incidentally, and your first illustration.

It was later in my high-school career that an emotional young sportswriter for the local paper tabbed one of my defensive plays a "crunching slash" and that my father, Sid, became inspired to blurb my career along. At that time Dad was just a stay-at-home drunk who read *Photoplay, Woman's Day, TV Guide* and other such magazines as my mother could afford to buy after a day's work as a roustabout for the Falfurias Oil and Drilling Company. The spirit of those publications and Dad's stubborn dream that I should be college-educated resulted in his loose-leaf notebook featuring that first, and, later, other clippings. The volume remained thin (only Lamar Tech showing interest in my athletic and academic future) until Dad blurbed me a little more on some long-distance phone calls. Eventually I was established as Mr. Crunch of South Texas.

"Hey there, Crunch!" called the dizzy coeds of Northwestern University as I later strolled those melancholy walkways beside Lake Michigan.

In truth, in my college days I was a walking blurb.

Until the varsity's first game I enjoyed reputation without the necessity of performance, but then I gamely led the kickoff team downfield to receive for my trouble a busted kneecap. Fortune only smiled, though, and some mindless editorialist for the campus paper later wrote that the school's season would have been far better that year "had good old Crunch Neal been playing."

That blurb, despite the fact that my knee never quite worked anymore, kept my athletic scholarship intact until after graduation. It taught me, too, the power of the blurb.

Like all college kids of my sickly generation I was later preparing dossiers so that I could enter the Business Establishment. My advantage over others became eminently clear: I had blurb power, they didn't. Coaches, wealthy alumni who worked in banks and warehouses, all those PR men and sportswriters were enlisted as contributors of recommendations. My portfolio bulged with non sequiturs and superlatives, all calculated to dismay employers, and I became a salesman in Manhattan.

The computer writing this isn't programmed to supply you with too many personal details. My sex life, hygiene, physical charm: all that has no proper place here, though, of course, you may surmise.

I also move at a swift pace to spare you an excess of Literary Style. Some of my wit will undoubtedly show itself (I programmed this lovely, whirring dinosaur, after all), but like all success stories this must run swift and true.

From salesman to show biz: a simple and obvious move. Only the things that could be blurbed—and packaged, as they say in Manhattan—could be sold, and knowing that I moved along into the executive hierarchy. I packaged actors and singers, for instance, with absolutely zero talent—having found that some of them lent themselves to the blurb. One guy had sideburns down to his shoulders—the longest sideburns in the history of the cabaret, really—and so I blurbed his sideburns, certainly not his pedestrian tones, and made a fortune for both him and my agency.

We were a wildcat Madison Avenue outfit, selling everything. And I had the knack, the quick flash of phrase (I wrote things on my napkins at Sardi's, in taxicabs, in the silence of my lonely room night and day) that moved the goods off the shelves. In those plush Eisenhower years, I finally bought out the senior partners, moved us into Fifth Avenue offices we couldn't afford, and installed the first part of our computer system.

(This thing is a beast, but we can store twenty million myriad blurbs in it and tell ourselves that we can't do without it.)

Anyway, I blurbed myself—continually and in various happy ways.

I fancied singing. Anybody who doesn't fancy himself a pop singer has no imagination at all. Soon, armed with a string of blurbs, I was the featured soloist—I was so bad that I had to hire two guitars, a pipe organ, and a tuba to accompany me—in the Blue Meany down in the Village. While my voice was insipid, my lyrics caught on because of their brevity and punch and I was eventually hailed as a serious young poet, truly deep and meaningful (that was a blurb), who spoke out against war, illness, and long working hours. My words, void of the banging rhythms and oom-pahs, were set down in a thin volume, and it, in turn, was blurbed heavily and scored. A minor best seller. I could have stopped there and had my own melodious identity.

But I founded the Neal Blurb Service.

I stop the computer at this point to feed it the contents of my desk memo pad right here in front of me. It should give testimony to my expanding influence, my busy success, and the pulse of my day.

Item: An order for 1,200,000 more Japanese-made blurb pins.

Item: Letter from a teeny-bopper in Cincinnati who wants to personally blurb Vladimir Nabokov.

Item: Article clipped from *Consumer's Report* and reprinted in *Changing Times* which begins, "Beware of the limitations of the famous Neal Blurb Service . . ."

Item: Draft of my letter to James Michener: "Dear Jim, Please try to limit your future blurbs to 2500 words or less. There is a significant technological reason for this in our highly computerized . . ."

Item: Note from my secretary to take my Vitamin C and hormones.

Item: The design for my newest inspiration, the bronze *Good Housekeeping* seal, which can be worn around the necks of thousands of Mothers who feel that housewifery has no rewards.

My early suc suc suc
(The computer anticipates, at times, and has to be started over.)

My early success in the Blurb Business was established in the worlds of publishing and literature.

Books, one might say, are hardly published and then reviewed and then bought by a discerning public which takes into account what the critics had to say. Hardly. Long before I entered the business, books were packaged. That is, a publisher spread around a few advance copies of a book he intended to publish, paid or otherwise induced Big-Time Reviewers to comment—usually favorably, but preferably in some controversial manner —and then staged a publicity drama. The pre-review system made every book look like a winner. Hence, The Package.

I offered all publishing houses my refined and computerized aid. Neal would come up with Bigger Names and Better Blurbs.

The Quality Lit game proved a fertile field. Everyone agreed to blurb everyone else—and throw in an occasional literary prize—if only they, in turn, were blurbed. Thus, Lionel Trilling blurbed Hans Habe who blurbed Dennis Hopper who blurbed ("Groovy Critic!") Trilling. Robert Penn Warren appreciated Andy Lytle ("Sho Nuff Stuff!") who raved over Allen Tate who thought very highly of Warren. Norm Mailer liked Jimmy Baldwin who adored Ken Kesey who dug Susie Sontag. Et cetera.

So among all the activities of the Neal Service—and this included plugging movies, appliances, cars, suburban developments, vacation resorts, sporting equipment, and exotic foods—we found our zenith in the World of Letters.

Naturally ra ra. (Excuse, again, please.)

Naturally I didn't stop there. The Single Greatest Conception in the History of Blurbing was my idea to blurb all people everywhere: the big name, the no name, the rich and poor, the glamorous and the snerd, regardless of race, creed, or national origin.

Thus, the Cornucopia of Blurb.

Mickey Mantle blurbs Frankie Avalon who blurbs Elmo Roper who blurbs Ed Sullivan who blurbs Herbert Marcuse who blurbs Bobo Rockefeller who blurbs the H. R. Block Corporation.

It was during this period of staggering company growth—I paid the lease on that Fifth Avenue property for a hundred years—that a simple formula came to me. People could wear their blurbs! If ever a man could manage to get himself endorsed in any way whatsoever, we would print up thousands of Blurb Buttons very much like those worn during election campaigns. Actually, a man needed only one—the one he wore on his own lapel and which made him a walking advertisement for himself—but we found customers who filled every drawer in their home with our emblems. It became an instant Status Symbol and in many cases almost a necessity. Consider the young down-and-out thespian who spent his days at stage doors and tryouts looking for a big break, but who turned to us and was soon wearing a button such as this one:

Most customers paid handsomely for their blurbs, I found, yet I turned no man away. And that simple housewife with her *Good Housekeeping* seal dangling over the kitchen sink was just as important to my final vision as anything else.

We sup sup. (All right, another pause. Right here on my memo pad I'm noting that my secretary should contact the computer adjustment analyst once more on Monday morning.)

We supplied an old prostitute, once, I was going to say, with blurbs from King Farouk, Errol Flynn, and the entire Santos Soccer Team. Think that didn't lift her sagging spirits?

Now da da

Nowadays the system booms and the Neal Service inspires new fronts.

I suffer not the slightest jealousy of those who steal and expand on my ideas.

> THE VERMONT BLURBERS CONFERENCE
> A summer Writing Program with the Accent
> on Leisure Hours and featuring a staff of
> Editors, Children's Authors, & Old Professors.
> LEARN THE ART OF THE BLURB IN OUR WORKSHOP SESSIONS!

Ebony Magazine will soon run a "Blurb Your Favorite Honky" contest.

> TOMBSTONE BLURBS, INCORPORATED
> "Solid Rock Statements!"
> Epitaphs at $10 Down & $10 a Month
> From a Distinguished List of Contributors

Curriculum Announcement, Fall, 1973: The MFA Program in Creative Blurbs will begin at UCLA. (Earn a Master of Fine Arts degree at this fine campus in the art of capsule criticism. Veterans invited.)

The philosophy behind all this is upbeat. Life is filled with the mediocre, the mundane, and people often become mired in indifferent jobs or routines, lost, adream, unappreciated and forgotten. Usually somewhere, someplace in their lives, someone cared for them, however, and the Neal Service can find that person and get a blurb from him. For a nominal fee, the Service can even muster a word from someone distinguished and widely known and recognized in the media.

The spirit of the blurb, after all, dispels life's bitterness, cuts through the complicated encumbrance of language ra and doles out a good phrase for everything zora taba dinky. The living and the dead get blurbed ra and in the great movement of the stars zella shantih I recall Three Rivers, the walkways abba beside Lake Michigan, the days before I found my calling and success in the lives of men shantoo villi casa more tonderoga goodie goodie good good good.

A Cook's Tale

> But greet harm was it, as it thoughte me,
> That on his shyne a mormal hadde he.
> For blankmanger, that made he with the best.
> —Chaucer

"Em, I'll bet that's right! I'll bet you make your old man wash dishes at home, huh?" he called across the chopping table toward the girl. His voice accomplished its broad rasp, the sound everyone expected from him, booming above the constant metallic pitch of spoons and skillets. He was taking his daily turn around the kitchen, barking at his workers, but in this last exchange, a moment before repeating the raillery for a third time, he sensed that he should have stopped.

"Look, he just studies," the girl answered him. Then, again: "He studies very hard!" She spat out this last, biting down on her lip, tears rising in her eyes so that she turned away in embarrassment. Turning, though, she collided with the other cook, Mr. Avery, then broke away and ran, leaving the two of them standing dumbfounded. She slammed through the storeroom door and the bolt clicked after her.

"What?" the Swede asked Mr. Avery. "What'd I do?"

"Don't talk to her about her husband today," Mr. Avery answered grimly. Mr. Avery had been there longer than anyone, but from time to time, being restless, he had gone out West or up to Chicago to work with his uncle so that, in time, he had lost seniority. He turned out all the basic dishes, though, and the two, he and the Swede, were good friends because the hard duty of the kitchen made rank matter little.

"Her husband flunked his exam this morning," he explained to the Swede. "He'll have to stay at the university another semester. That's all. They'll let him try again this spring, I think."

"The big degree, huh?" the Swede asked, pretending ignorance.

"Aw, sure. It don't mean the boy's dumb. 'Course not. Lots of boys flunk them exams first time around then do okay later. Sure!"

Back at the stoves the Swede watched a big pan of potatoes boil and roll. He stared into the combustion absently, concerned with his indiscretion. He hadn't meant it. He had faked it too hard for once. It was just the way in the kitchen, between everyone, how they all had to be: always a little too noisy, slapping the utensils around like a bunch of old men whacking cards down in a tonk game, always vulgar to excess. And old style: its origins weren't clear, he knew, but it was the way. He watched the water as if something hid there, his face blank and adream, his thoughts going off toward strange unlikely latitudes where he knew no one would guess to find him, to lost continents, Palmyra, steep mountain roads, cities beneath the sea.

When Em came back from the storeroom and took her position at her dishwashing machine, he went over and stood behind her. He watched the rhythmic glide of her arms and shoulders as she stacked plates and he waited, steam rising in a cloud toward the fluorescent tubes above them, until he imagined her composure had come back.

When he apologized he saw her head nod only slightly in acknowledgment. Foolishly, then, he added something else: " 'Pain she was capable of causing me; joy, never. Pain alone kept my tedious attachment alive.' "

When she turned on him, smiling, he realized his mistake. "That quotation," she said, accusation in her tone. "Where's it from?"

"I don't suppose I know," he managed to say.

"You don't know? Really? If you were in my sweet crowd, you'd know. Snob value and all, I mean. That sounded so literate and so calculated, you know."

He had never really listened to her talk. "Yes," he said, hoping to hear her speak one more time, "I guess I just picked it up. A long time ago, probably."

"And you don't honestly remember the source? Marvelous!"

"The comics, maybe," he suggested.

"What exactly now? Pain keeps them attached? What a nice turn."

"I didn't mean anything ugly about your husband a while ago," he offered, trying to end it. He saw that she looked at him in a peculiarly direct way. Unable to keep his eyes in hers, he gazed up into the gathering steam. Proust in the kitchen, he said to himself. Ridiculous. So pretentious of me that I damned well deserve to get caught.

"I can't get over it," she said, scooting a stack of plates a few inches down and starting a new pile near her left arm. "I've never really heard of anyone who doesn't carefully include footnotes and references. But don't let me tease you. You don't see what I mean, do you?"

"Not exactly," he said, understanding fully. "Why is it? Does your husband study literature?"

"Oh, no. History and economics," she answered, still

stacking, still watching him. She peered into his eyes in the way a woman hadn't done in years. Fighting certain considerations, he switched to something else, conjuring up an image of his chair at home, of Berta's old quilt draped over it, of his brass ashtray and the table with water-ring markings. He tried to remember the book he was reading, but couldn't. No, he told himself. Never mind all that. I'd like to go someplace and sit with her and talk. Talk for a long time. He fought to regain the conversation.

"And you're working while he goes to school," he said flatly, a little stupidly. He knew this all too well.

"Sure. You know that," she told him.

"How long now? Let's see. Three years, isn't it?"

"In June, yes. I was a carrier first, you know. I thought it would be better upstairs in those quiet corridors. The kitchen is so noisy. But I didn't like being around the nurses."

"What was wrong? They weren't nice to you?"

"Oh, I just looked so sloppy. All my trays and food stains. I finally decided just to stay down here in the mess."

"I've got some potatoes on," he said by way of excuse. "We can talk again sometime. Sometime later. Right now I've got to shape up."

When he was a few steps off she called out something which he didn't hear and he turned for her to repeat it. "I said I've got your number now," she called. "Quoting me such a thing! I'm going to ask Raymond who you've been reading!"

Back at his stove he wiped the burners clean, hung up his knives and spatulas, and glanced into the big vat where the boiling potatoes knocked against the sides crazily. The motor on the conveyor belt buzzed unevenly, one of its gaskets loose, and he felt his hands trembling.

On a day eight years before this, a Saturday in April of 1954, John Olaf had bought the entire Modern Library, all four hundred-odd titles at a discount of 10 percent, a concession of the publishers, and his wife, Berta, had packed up and fled to St. Paul. The Swede's luck, however, as always, didn't hold: back she came after three days, armed with all the proxy indignation of her relatives and old friends in Minnesota, and sworn never to let him forget, ever, his pride and folly.

"Our whole savings," she would complain. "Not even counting the cost of shelves. You'll never build all them shelves!"

"You'll not mention shelves one more time," he would warn her, and something in his voice, a strange severity, would compel her to stop. Later, of course, she would begin in another direction.

"Alphabetical!" she might suddenly snap, ridiculing him. "Pah! Nobody in this town, in the whole world probably, reads alphabetical!"

"I do," he would tell her with the same authority.

"It'll be scrambled up that way," she would argue. "Now even chronological I could maybe understand, John, but hardly alphabetical!"

"Leave me alone!" he would say. "I already read this page twice and couldn't understand a word for your yellin' at me!"

During his sixteen years the kitchen at University Hospital had scarcely changed, keeping a staff of eighteen, two shifts, morning and evening, the latter shift having the fewer workers. Besides Mr. Avery and himself there were seven women at the dishwashing machines who also scrubbed pans, stacked silverware and plates, and others who were salad helpers and carriers or who worked around the conveyor belt. Mrs. Poling, the dietitian, supplied the Swede with a weekly menu, but mostly confined herself to chores upstairs or in the county schools where she occasionally gave health lectures. Others worked less directly with the kitchen: certain nurses, for instance, or the men on the supply dock. It was a big kitchen, remodeled once in 1950 and painted fresh every two summers, full of noise, and for sixteen years the Swede, for all his personal alterations, had ordered everyone with a sharp indifference. He drove them toward accurate schedules and timing; speed and good timing, he admonished them like a sergeant, were the important things.

At home the timing was forever scuttled in Berta's lackluster housekeeping so that he felt sharply, always, even before his purchase of the books, the schizophrenia of life at work and of life at the apartment. She wore her rolled socks like drooping flags of surrender. Having never bothered since the first years of their marriage with stays or supports, her body puffed under a cotton dress like bread overloaded with yeast. She urged him to always eat his big meal at work and offered him only frozen foods and dull muffins in the evenings. For years, too, it was money. Then Mr. Avery, at last, took leave once too often so that the Swede ascended to top cook. Berta relaxed somewhat, drew up budgets at first, then forgot even those. He felt himself altogether divided: the kitchen thrived, the apartment slept. When he walked in the town, across those wide expanses near the stadium where, on certain afternoons, Wisconsin and Notre Dame and California came to battle, he sensed the vitality. Students banged through the snow with zest, jostled him at the counters where he drank his beers en route home, argued with enthusiasm in booths and jumped up excitedly, yelling, laughing, and springing off toward important academic matters.

The bookstores seemed great world banks packed with crucial bartering and visionary shoppers. He sensed his intrusion in these places, especially on his noon visits. He would eat hurriedly or perhaps even sneak a few mouthfuls during preparation so that he could walk across campus and peek at a few titles before the one o'clock whistle. He stood among students wrapped in their sweet-smelling wool and cashmere sweaters giving off his onion odors, his frock, covered with beet drippings or splashes of ketchup, dangling out of his mackinaw. Titles and book jackets amazed him. For more than a year he showed up in the town's three bookstores twice or three times a week to trace that great red sausage of his forefinger down the rows, reading blurbs and names. At noon and after work before going home to the apartment, standing there as sales rang up all around him, nodding stupidly, sometimes, to students passing in the aisles, he would stand, eyes focusing slowly, as if he read unbelievable recipes and strange and terrible formulas on the covers. He never so much as looked inside them, just waited, mentally gathering his resources together, his energies and emotional ingredients. And he said nothing to Berta all this time. What was there to say? He knew of no sure starting place.

Finally a new clerk, a flippant little student with glasses who came to work that spring of 1954, made him so angry that he bought the whole set of books. "I was only kidding, buddy," the kid said after the Swede had affirmed he would buy them all. "It was just a joke, that suggestion."

"It don't matter," the Swede said. "What's the matter? You think I can't write a check so big?"

They arrived in three boxes from New York City, postpaid, and that day Berta declared that he had lost his head. She took the late afternoon coach to St. Paul, pointing her finger and making a considerable number of threats in the station, but already her dynasty was under siege. She could never really threaten him again.

Though after *The Education of Henry Adams*, the first book on the list, he wavered. He sat zombielike in the big chair, her quilt draped across his knees and the book resting on top of that, staring out dumbly. He hadn't understood ten passages in the whole book. For days afterward the hospital kitchen seemed a nightmare; he cut his thumb badly with a paring knife, something he hadn't done in ten years or more, and once salted the stew twice, vigorously too, so that it had to be thrown out. The second reading was no better. At this point Berta seemed to see her advantage, forgave him the expense of the books, called him back into the abyss of television programs and long early-evening naps, but he decided to give the document a last try. At the university library he looked up Sumner, Gladstone, Palmerston and the many unyielding historical allusions in encyclopedias. Then he returned to the book and read it a third time and one morning, perched on the bedside, drawing on his socks, he remarked, "Schools are wicked things, Bert. I agree with Henry there. Just a fragment of a fragment is all we're ever goin' to know." Berta raised up stiffly, gave him a momentary look, wondered who Henry was, and returned to her sleep unconscious of what he had actually said.

He never romanticized his accomplishment. His reading remained painfully slow. He faced impossible alphabetical barriers and at the end of his first year he had moved only beyond Dante into the midst of Dostoyevsky, encountering between them, somewhere, despair. He took to drinking something more bracing than his afternoon beers, and Berta, frustrated and hurt, left him twice, staying once in St. Paul for three weeks. When they had no more money she felt she couldn't leave him anymore; he buried himself in a second enthusiastic reading of Sherlock Holmes and ignored her.

In time the initial artifices slipped away. He disregarded the elaborate system of shelves he had resolved to build in the bedroom and simply stored the books, still boxed, in the rear of a closet. He moved beyond ownership to partial possession. His role in the kitchen became more and more difficult and he often wanted to confess his project to Mr. Avery, but didn't. It was left for him to give himself away.

Out of the kitchen Emma Bryant was a thing transformed, a young woman of graceful affectation and a real talker. He tried to imagine the apartment which she described for him: her husband's volumes edging up the panels of their den, his pipe rack and walnut humidor, the Japanese lamp, the rug they had bought in twelve long installments. They sat in a little bar east of the campus while he listened to her speak of the rug. "I couldn't live without it," she made clear. "It makes everything so quiet. Isn't it just awfully important to have everything quiet after that damned kitchen?" He agreed: yes, everything needed to be quiet after such a ruckus. She told how she slept on the rug, how she took off everything except her slip and curled below the phonograph, her arm under her face, her thumb wedged between the pages of a novel or some political paperback. Raymond insisted that she read and she tried, she told the Swede, but her body always submitted to the rug before a dozen pages. As she talked he imagined her watching him while they worked in the kitchen, while he yelled above the rising clatter, waving his big red hands, breaking the backs and wings and thighs of chickens and pitching them into steaming vats. Nearly all the hospital food was boiled. Boiling itself, he mused, sitting there beside her, was a war of jangled atoms, a dreadful churning, a low note of chaos amidst the steady discord of the kitchen.

She had consented to a beer more easily than he had imagined. Moreover, the asking was simple. They sat on the same side of the booth, her hip pressed on his. She drank off the first schooner like a sailor but fondled the second slowly, turning it in her long fingers, her eyes adream, talking incessantly.

"It's all bearable," she was saying, "because I know I'm going off somewhere to a nice white house, all carpeted, and to a neighborhood all soft with so many beautiful trees, and that I'm going to have people saying very soft nice things in my living room. Anything is bearable, I believe, if I can just accomplish that wonderful luxury of silence. Don't you think so?"

"Yes, that's right," he put in.

"Raymond's going to pass this next time, too," she went on. "In spite of those professors. Oh, they've been such asses. They've ground him all the way down now. He used to be such a shark. Had a bite like a razor. Had all those wonderful radical ideas, you know. Only they've sat on him so hard for such a long time that they've compromised him. I don't suppose you know what I mean. But he's so careful now. He weighs everything he says." She sipped at her beer. "He's such a wonderfully careful person now, I mean." This last she added, he knew, because she didn't want to sound too hard. But of course she was. He thought of the harried faces of the older graduate students in the bookstores, remembered their faces as deep maps of weariness, and supposed her husband was one of them. He didn't know whether to be happy or sad that her marriage suffered. Their waitress slapped the pinball machine with the palms of her hands, tilting it, and when she turned away toward them he called her over and ordered a last round.

He found himself unable to speak his mind with her and contented himself with listening. Her transformation seemed nearly complete; her voice danced full of flights and laughter, so that he imagined her off in a drawing room among the Guermantes or with Thackeray's brittle socialites. Highly pretentious, he decided. But he didn't care. In time, he thought, I'll make the necessary revelations. I'll take her hand one evening, perhaps, and say—oh, it'll probably sound so damned stupid —that I've read from Adams to Zola and that I'm in the midst of the giant editions now. Almost nine years, Em, I'll say, and I'm not even reading alphabetically anymore.

"Sensitivity," she was saying. As she spoke she removed a small tube of lanolin from her purse, pressed some into her palm, and massaged her hands and wrists gently. "I sometimes think we're walking a tightrope, both Ray and myself. I stand around those machines all day with Mrs. Brogan and Mrs. Tate, you know, and I'm finally numb, I can't think or talk anymore. We go out to a party occasionally where there are Raymond's very important professors and I just have to muster everything I've got to smile and talk with them. I just know that some evening I'm going to come out with a good solid crap-it-all! Mr. Avery's delicate phrase! Or I'll start wiping up after everyone's glasses. Can't you imagine it? But I want to be sensitive. I damned well insist on it! And *wanting* to keep on feeling and thinking makes a difference doesn't it? I'm not completely vulgar after three years, I hope. Am I?" He moved his lips into a smile, ready to answer, but she reached over, grasped two of his fingers in her hand, and pressed hard. "You're so damned strong," she told him, switching abruptly. "I watch you in the kitchen sometimes. I saw you lift that big lard can yesterday, for instance. I noticed you didn't even change your expression."

Such adolescent flattery. Such elementary tactics. His senses flew apart and he curled his hand in hers; he was Vronsky meeting Anna and Dante rising out of flame to embrace Beatrice.

In the street, walking back toward the hospital, the snow piled up at curbs like bundles of old dirty laundry awaiting spring, he studied her face. Her most impressive transformation was physical: her mouth seemed brighter, her eyes deeper. They went on talking until they reached the edge of a practice field where she again pressed his hand. He watched her trudge away, following a path children had worn in the snow with their sleds and disks, until she passed out of sight through the trees toward the student apartment building. Then he turned, went back almost the length of the town to his place, ate a bowl of tepid soup, spoke a few courteous and superficial sentences to Berta, and sat down heavily in his accustomed chair. He couldn't read. In less than an hour his copy of Plutarch had slipped down into the crook of his elbow and he wheezed slightly in sleep.

During the next weeks he seemed only a spectator in the kitchen and often heard his own voice with alarm as it rose over Mr. Avery's short knife strokes at the salad bench. "Oregano!" he would shout. It sounded silly, like an entrance line at an opera or, on other occasions, like a surgeon calling for some important instrument at an operation. His mind, meanwhile, traveled back to every moment in that booth, to her every word and gesture.

A second opportunity finally came. Part of the hospital staff, the older foreign doctors in residence, decided on a banquet for themselves, and the Swede was put in charge of the meal. Six others, including Em, volunteered for overtime. He informed Berta that he would be very late, midnight or after.

At the close of the banquet the kitchen was quiet except for the hum of the dishwashing machines. The Swede took off his apron, threw on his coat, then went out to the parking lot, started the motor of his old Plymouth, and brought it around to the loading dock. Then he came back inside, took off his overcoat again, rubbed his large red hands together briskly, and went over to Em. She had stayed, as he knew she would, until the others had gone. He helped her take the last load out of the machine.

"I've got my car," he said, casually, as if there were no premeditation. "You won't have to walk home in the snow. I left the motor going so it'll be warm."

At the door he helped her with her parka. As he flipped off the light switches he looked back over his shoulder at the darkened room: pans and spoons and knives on their hooks, everything glowing in the light slanting through the windows from a streetlamp.

They drove for more than an hour, going by dreary winter fields, occasionally passing another car, its noise muffled by the snowpacked roads. When they stopped, later, at the edge of the stadium's shadow, she didn't resist. Though the front seat was awkward, she moved as he directed, her hands caressing the long red muscles of his upper arms, her mouth whimpering softly at his chin. Then she laughed out loud and the laugh trailed off into an extended giggle. "What's the matter?" he wanted to know.

"I'm sorry," she said, still giggling. "But you smell like vegetable soup. Honest. Oh, I'm sorry. I couldn't figure

out what it was for the longest!" He felt exhausted and
very foolish. Onions, turnips, carrots, all the fluids of his
body, he knew, had been given to her and he wondered
if she felt anything at all, if she regarded him as more
vegetable than animal, as more animal than man. He
came right to the brink of telling her about his reading,
but couldn't do it. What, after all, would that have to do
with anything? Nothing, he knew. Nothing.

Winter passed and cornfields rose up green out of the
midwestern bog. While Raymond Bryant entombed himself at the university library, Em and the Swede took
long drives. They made discoveries: a wild grove of apple trees, a small park in a nearby town replete with
bandbox and mineral-water spring, even a hillside. In
such a flat, uninterrupted country this seemed their real
accomplishment. On this hillside, in all these places, they
made love. But they talked less as time went on. At
home, his reading almost stopped. He drank more heavily and felt bound and helpless.

One morning at breakfast Berta pulled her chair next
to his while he ate his eggs. It was not yet six in the
morning. Afterward, she would go back to bed and sleep
until midmorning. "You remember, John," she asked,
"when you first came back from the war fifteen, sixteen
years ago?"

He said that he remembered.

"How you was nervous and all?"

"That's right," he said.

"You said you wasn't going to stay no army cook. You
recall sayin' that?"

He gazed across the room, nibbled at a bacon strip,
and nodded.

"We were makin' up so much lost time, you recall.

You were the biggest man. Handsome. But you had such nerves. I don't think I really understood that, John, at the time. I thought it was the bombs in Normandy, you know, or all the things you wanted to forget. I was real careful not even to talk to you about it. We went on for a long time like that, you recall. Years. Then we had our fusses and when you bought your books I went off mad. But, John, I think you got a lot of good out of them books. Really. I'm even glad now."

"These are good eggs, Bert," he said. "You finally decided to put some milk in them like I told you."

"That's right."

"I usually eat my real breakfast after I get to work, you know, Bert."

"I know it. I realize that." She watched him drink off his coffee and wipe his lips. At his left hand was the morning newspaper, still folded, and the new book from his box: William H. Prescott. "John," she said, "you shouldn't worry none. I figure you're drinkin' so much late at night because you've got things on your mind, but I want you to know that I understand about you. I know it ain't entirely nerves. I know you've had a big desire all your life."

"I'm a silly man," he told her.

"That's all right," she said. "I don't care about that."

In the rattle of the kitchen he let his mind go blank in all the steam and heavy food odors, but at intervals thoughts came to him. He remembered Berta in the short print dresses she had worn during the war. Berta: she had fallen out of time into the indolent flats of sad routine while minutes and hours still vexed him, still tugged urgently at his apron. Often, after that brief communication over breakfast, his old feelings for her weighted him, a ballast of sorrow in his flight.

He went, once, to the university library where he sat

at a table watching the students. He saw how they fenced their desks with books, reading first from one then another, then making notes impressively. His own helter-skelter venture struck him as infinitely absurd. One student especially drew his attention: a small, bent, older-looking young man with heavy spectacles laboring in a sea of manuscripts and periodicals. Raymond Bryant, he imagined. He looked down suddenly at his hands spread out before him and studied them as though a message, written in a strange and mystic language, might be read there.

Toward midnight one evening at the apartment, sitting in the big chair, his books in disarray around his feet, newspaper strewn on the water-marked table, ashtray bulging, he reached for a drink, but drew back his hand carefully. No, he decided. No more of that. He slipped into a light jacket and walked the eight blocks downtown. Streetlamps and store windows drew him into their light like a moth. Beyond the university lawn with its webs of sidewalk, the clock tower peered down solemnly, its luminous face a hole in the sky. Before him lay the street, empty, like a relic of memory. In all his years in this town, in all his days of going by these familiar shops and markers on his way to work at the kitchen, he had never felt so accused by their doleful stare. Em, he wanted to say, I need someone to talk to. I really do.

He walked slowly home again. Though he tried, he couldn't think logically about her. Of course she wasn't the one. Of course he allowed himself to serve her image. Besides, she wore a grim falsity; her ambitions were absurd, hollow, even ugly. The quiet neighborhood and white house: pah! Her body served her husband's career by its devotion to the kitchen, but betrayed him in love. But what of all this? He didn't care.

In all the world there was her only. She seemed his only possible breakthrough.

He saw her infrequently through the early spring and in April, though they managed to have Wednesdays off together, Raymond usually managed to spoil a possible meeting. They stayed careful while at work, speaking to each other very little, knowing how fast the university and town gossip circles worked. And except for their lovemaking this reticence seemed to carry over into their times together. It was because she contented herself with giving him simple definition, the one she had reserved for him since the start, thinking of him as a strong man, a physical cushion against her academic world, a man virile and keen at forty-two who could swing those fifty-gallon cans on his shoulder. He didn't object. But why was he so afraid? He probed himself with this question after their every meeting. Once they drove out to an arbor in the countryside where he had gone with Berta years before, a spot where deer often came late in the evenings. She spread out a picnic and when they had finished eating they walked down a dirt road, Em with her shoes off and him with his shirt thrown over his back. "Your skin," she said. "It's like a beet. So red! It actually glows!" And as she stopped and rubbed her palms up the length of his chest, his thoughts sped along crazily to Thoreau, to Santayana, to old Walt Whitman. Stupe, he told himself. Idiot. Jerk.

In the kitchen one May afternoon she came to him, smiling, and announced, "Raymond passed his examination. Isn't it wonderful?" No, he wanted to say, it isn't so wonderful, but he said yes, yes it was a happy thing for everyone.

"What's the matter?" she asked him.

He couldn't say anything.

"Don't you see?" she said. "I won't have to work anymore! It'll all be over soon! Three years and it's all finished. Completely!"

"You do need to get out of this place," he admitted.

"Oh, god, yes! Some morning soon I'm going to get out of bed and after breakfast I'm going to sprawl out on that rug and sleep the whole day."

As he peeled an additional carrot she followed him down the row of stoves and watched him toss it into the stew. "We'll celebrate tonight, of course. Raymond agreed. You'll come, won't you?"

"I couldn't do that. Don't be silly."

"Of course you could! There'll be so many instructors, some of his professors, so many friends dropping in. Who'll know you?"

"I couldn't do it, Em."

"Oh, but I want you to!"

Why? He wondered what Emma ever wanted. Really wanted. "I'd be a sore thumb," he argued.

"I may not come back to the kitchen after Friday," she said without too much mercy. "And we may be leaving town. Who knows? There's bound to be job offers now. How many hours will we have left? Oh, I want you there! Honestly. Can't you do it?"

That evening Berta called him to the phone. "There's a drunk lady on here," she told him. "She knows your name. You know any drunk ladies?"

He took the phone and heard Emma laughing on the other end of the line. Berta stood by, watching his mouth work toward speech, then moved away and left him alone in the hallway. He listened to Emma giggling and heard the invitation urged and repeated. "All right," he said. "I'll make an excuse. I'll be right over." She laughed bell-like off in some far away corner of the night.

The windows of the student apartment buildings were mostly open on the warm spring evening and on the terrace the Swede stopped, leaned forward, and listened. A mother called her small Cathleen to bed and someone's radio reported a fire in Des Moines. A baby wailed. He went unsuccessfully into three doorways and read a total of eighteen mailboxes before finding himself within earshot of the party. At the door he knocked softly and was quickly admitted by a bearded young man named Rodney who offered him a glass of vodka and 7-Up. An old professorial gentleman slumped in one corner strumming a mandolin for two admiring young ladies. On the phonograph: drums. Another girl stood waiting outside what the Swede took to be the bathroom door. He acknowledged the Japanese lamp, Raymond's walnut humidor, the often-discussed rug, and, on it, Emma. She wore several strands of fancy beads: jade, opal, onyx, something else red, so many that they fell down over her shoulders and elbows as she lay there. She looks, he thought, like a salad. As Rodney ushered him toward some ice cubes, he nodded toward the beads and they rattled in answer.

A long evening, he decided. It's going to be a long one. He drank off his vodka and allowed Rodney to pack his glass with more cubes.

Somehow, before he emerged from replenishing his glass back where the bottles sat in the breakfast nook, he had mentioned his readings to this bearded young man and had managed to offend him. He didn't fully understand how this happened. Already the first drink worked on him.

"Plutarch!" Rodney exclaimed. "Hey, nice. Real ritzy. Wow!"

"Yes, the lives, you know," the Swede said. It came out even more stupidly than his first remarks. He made

A Cook's Tale

a mental note to say nothing more to anyone, especially not to this young man.

"Oh, dad, I had you pegged for the gypsy-scholar type, you know. You turn out to be a bloody classicist, though, huh? Well, we'll just see about that!"

The Swede walked away. Finding the bathroom vacant, he went inside. He leaned against the lavatory and drank down his second glass, some undetermined liquor. Through the door he could hear modulations of voices followed by wild bursts of laughter. Jokes, he decided. They're telling stories. Then, for no particular reason, he began to count. One. He didn't know exactly why. Two. He only knew he had escaped to the bathroom in order to fortify himself. Three. And four. He wasn't really a drinking man, he realized. Already fixtures were beginning to jump up the walls. Five.

He bumped into Em briefly in the hallway outside. "That was your wife on the phone, wasn't it?" she asked, twining her fingers in her beads.

"That's right."

"I guess you think I've got a lot of guts calling like that."

"I've got some myself. I came, didn't I?"

"Get yourself something else to drink," she said. "We'll sit down together later on. I've got to call a neighbor about some ice right now."

In the living room the old gentleman with the mandolin stopped playing, leaned out toward him, and extended a hand. "Biddle here," he grunted. The Swede was obviously supposed to know Biddle.

He had been on the couch scarcely a minute when Rodney found him again. "I've got no use for the classics boys at any school," he said.

"That's okay," the Swede answered.

"I've seen the trouble in fifty schools if I've seen it

once. Everything has to go back to the Greeks. The New Criticism you take back to the goddamned Greeks. Everything. Symbolism. You leave no room for contemporary contribution, man. Don't you see that?"

The Swede didn't understand and said so. While Rodney directed criticism into his left ear, he twisted on the cushions, arched forward, and gazed down at his big hands. They seemed ridiculous: too large, so red that they appeared almost luminous, bright advertisements of a life among spoons and spatulas. Finally, with Rodney still talking, he made his way back into the breakfast nook. Em hadn't come back with the ice so he simply drank one straight this time.

He realized they were telling funny stories again in the living room. The laughter came in strong voice vote. Did they want him out of the room when they told jokes? He poured another Scotch in the bottle cap.

Emma passed through leaving two trays of ice in the sink, hurrying off, apparently toward something urgent. He wondered if he should have brought food. He saw nothing to eat anywhere.

Rodney cornered him again. "A spirit like Byron—you smother a spirit like that!" he affirmed this time, and went on to make several derogatory remarks about poetic formalism, whatever that was.

"Leave me alone, buddy," the Swede said, and he walked back into the living room again, standing at the edge of the crowd with Em.

"You look pretty potted already," she observed in a whisper.

"I think I'm hungry," he said. "Should I go down to the kitchen and make up a few hors d'oeuvres?"

"Oh, don't be silly! Sit down. Have you even met Raymond yet?"

"I'll meet him. Right at the moment I'm thinking about going down to the hospital kitchen."

"Sit down," she whispered sharply. "And not so loud. That's Biddle telling stories now."

Rodney was at his sleeve again. "You think I don't know how you classicists have control of English departments all over the country?" he complained.

"Look, buzz off," the Swede ordered him, trying to raise his voice to its authoritative kitchen quality and yet trying not to disturb Biddle's joke.

"You can't put me down," Rodney insisted. "I'm really on to your kind, aren't I? That's what's galling you!"

"You're mixed up and out of line," the Swede answered.

"Go mix me another sour, will you, Rod?" Emma whispered.

"I will go down to the kitchen," the Swede said. "Maybe I'll whip up some pizza. Something like that for a party."

"You don't have to!" Emma said aloud.

He suddenly had to get out. While everyone broke into laughter over Biddle's story, he made his way through them toward the door. Rodney, though, hung at his heels and out in the hallway beside the mailboxes continued to accuse and badger the Swede about things he really didn't understand or want to hear. Confused, feeling as though this bearded pursuer held him back, the Swede hit him in the mouth. It was a short punch, quick and deliberate, as if the Swede simply wanted to stick the putty of his big red fist into a widening crack. Since the door was still half open, several guests in the room saw the punch and came out into the foyer embarrassed and curious. "What's all this? What? Who started it?" Raymond Bryant wanted to know. The

Swede had his first real look at Em's husband: crew-cut, glasses, short and muscular.

"Why'd you do that?" Rodney kept asking in disbelief, not sure at all that academic argument should rightfully include such tactics. From time to time he released the two-handed grip he kept over his mouth and beard and spat on the tile below the mailboxes. "This from a classicist!" he whined during one spitting interval.

The Swede addressed the crowd in the doorway. "I'm going down to my kitchen and get everyone something nice to eat. What'd you like? Maybe some pizza? No good, huh? All right, I'll just surprise everybody. You'll see. Just get yourselves back inside and have a good time and I'll be back in a little while." Standing behind her husband in the doorway, Emma shrieked with laughter at the Swede's familiar style of instruction. This last statement, too, so much approximated threat that everyone generally complied and edged back into the apartment.

Rodney spat again and watched the Swede with growing apprehension. Raymond Bryant kept asking, "What? Who is this guy? Who're you?"

Going down the walk, the Swede still heard Em's laughter. It sounded as it had on the phone, far away, like a mocking distant bell.

Because he was still drunk and not thinking too clearly, he decided on bread. He rolled out several giant patties of dough, then began kneading them fervently. He squeezed and pulled and slapped with all his strength, marveled at his enthusiasm for the job, laughed out loud. "You just have to be in the mood for bread," he told the empty kitchen. "You have to get your old juices up." After shaping ten large loaves and placing them in pans, he went back to the storeroom and removed two pounds of butter from the big cooler. He switched on the dishwashing machines because he needed noise.

But after a few minutes sitting on his tall stool, waiting, he knew his mistake. Bread took a long time in the making, as much as five hours, and the party would be long over. Bread. He wondered why he had even thought of such a thing. "We used to eat fresh hot bread," he told the kitchen. "This was a long time ago. With mounds of butter. God, I remember how good it was." Who used to eat new bread with him? Berta? Or was this just a stray childhood memory? He swayed on the stool and seemed adrift, unable to think. Whatever, he told himself, no one at the party would understand. They didn't seem much like bread people. Pizza people, maybe, yes, but certainly not the fresh-hot-bread-with-butter-in-it sort. A dietary error, he allowed, borrowing Mrs. Poling's terminology.

He went back to the party only slightly more sober. Biddle had altered his reserve completely and played a spirited folk chord while everyone sang. "Heave 'em up and away we go!" they boomed at each other. "Way out to Cal-i-forn-ee-yo!" He stood near the edge of their circle trying to pick up the lyric and looking, meanwhile, for Em. The crowd had increased to nearly thirty.

He continued to sing with them, his voice surprisingly on key, while circling the room in search of Em. Finally, at the bedroom door, he saw her stretched out across the bed. He turned so that he faced the crowd, but so that he could see her too from the corner of his eye. While he joined them in another, he saw Rodney giving him a somewhat sheepish gesture, almost a greeting wave of the hand, from across the room. Old Biddle's transitions were without pause and everyone continued stubbornly.

When she looked up he was inside the room and had closed the door behind him. He stood at the edge of the bed watching her.

"You'd better unlock that door," she warned him.

"I didn't lock it."

"Well, you've got your nerve. I'll give you credit for that."

He didn't move, just stood looking at her, and because he had the nerve, because they both had it, because there was only the dare of that paper-thin apartment wall separating them from the others, perhaps, or because they were still warm with their liquor, his blood began to race through his veins. When he dropped down on the bed beside her she grabbed him and held on tightly.

Luckily, during the whole time that she held him, until they finished, no one came in. In spite of this, though, he took care to startle her. Toward the last of their embrace, he pulled her hair away from her ear and whispered: "Don't you know me, Emma sweet? I'm old Odysseus dressed like the beggar. I'm Zarathustra in a pudding mask." He felt her stiffen under him and saw her eyes widen, but closed her mouth with his hand before she could respond. "And we're really a couple of shady characters, you know. A couple of Medicis, Em. You know that? What'll ever become of us? We'll be left to poetry, I guess. What sort now? Let me think. A weary old line from Donne? 'Since you would save none of me, I bury some of you.' Appropriate? Well, probably not. But it came to mind. I haven't the time, of course, to really do us justice."

He began to talk in long compelling bursts, pacing the floor around the bedstead as he poured out on her a bombardment of allusion and borrowed metaphor and half-stilted poetic jumble, as he tried to say it all, to gather up all that he had been feeling. She sat up straight in the middle of the bed and looked at him with that old direct gaze of hers. She hadn't looked at him in such a way in months. "I can't stop," he said at last. "I can't stop talking. Speaking to you like this, lecturing you. I've already made a speech tonight, too, haven't I? Out there in the hallway everyone wondered who the hell I was. I'm sorry about that. And about this, too. I'm still making speeches. In fact, I feel like I might never stop."

But he did. She looked so weary and broken and he didn't want to hurt her, not at all. He straightened his clothes and went over to peek out of the door. "You wait a bit before you come out," he ordered her. "And good-bye, Em." As her lips formed a word, he slipped out, stood at the edge of the circle again, and added his voice to the increased volume of the singing. Finally, catching the spirit, he clapped his hands with the rhythm, laughed, and bellowed out loudly at phrases he could remember or anticipate. In a few minutes she followed him into the room, made her way along the wall avoiding anyone's eyes, and took refuge among the bottles back in the breakfast nook.

Sometime after midnight he made his way back toward the hospital. His loaves had risen nicely and he slipped them into the oven and soon breathed in their fragrance as they baked.

Afterward, he went home. Carrying a warm loaf under each arm, he walked along crisply, humming one of the night's tunes.

The Arsons of Desire

One begins in familiar ways: a civil service test, a training school, and later the excitement of one's first fires and the fancy of wearing the uniform and helmet. I began this way, becoming a fireman, setting out to serve the citizens while serving myself some needed solitude, but lately I'm ambushed with dreams and visions. This sort: I'm in the company of a beautiful girl in a room filling with smoke. We exchange a love glance, her fingers brush my face, we start to embrace, then, disconcerted by the smoke, we look for a way out. She takes my hand as I lead her around the walls searching for a door; she wears a translucent gown, flowing like flame itself, and her dark hair spills over her shoulders. Then, the room stifling, we grope and panic; somewhere in the next few moments, terrified, our hands lose grip, and when I finally kick through the thin wall with my heavy rubber boot she fails to escape with me and I lose her.

Visions of a high blaze now and lovely lost women: I believe, lately, that I'm carrying disaster with me; my mind is catching fire.

This is the station house. In the old days bachelor firemen usually lived at the stations, but now I'm one of the few in all Chicago who continue. Others here have families, work in three shifts—twenty-four hours on, forty-eight off—but I stay near the alarms, I must, and attend every call. My bed in the dorm upstairs is in a homey corner: books, clock radio, my boots and britches stacked and ready. Downstairs are the big Seagrave trucks: the two quads, the ladder truck, the new snorkel, the new pump truck with its shiny deck gun, and the Cadillac rescue unit. Over here is the classroom, the kitchen, and the rec hall with Ping-Pong and television. The office and alarm systems are near the front door and in the rear are repair shops, storage rooms, and the garage where we keep the boats and drags. Sometimes our station is involved in dragging Lake Michigan or the river, but I've traded for other duties—I do considerable cleaning and mopping up around here—so that I can stay near the alarms. A dragging operation isn't a fire, after all; one gets a sore back, a head cold or sunburn, a soggy corpse, at best, and never peers into those bright and mystic flames.

Here we go: a two-alarm, the Lake Shore station and us.

Hanging on to number one truck with Captain Max, I curse the traffic as we whip into Lincoln Avenue. The siren begins to rev me up; I pull my suspenders tight, fasten my chin strap, and wonder who awaits me. In recent weeks it has been old Aunt Betty, the old family barber, a former high-school buddy of mine from up in Skokie, a girl I used to try to pick up in a bar on Gross Point Road. Strange, all strange: I can hardly wait.

Max is something: not a particularly good captain by the book and usually in trouble with the fire marshals because he's a real buster. We hit a building and he's off the truck, yelling, coupling hoses, and going in. I stomp in behind him, naturally, pulling the hose, my ax waving like his. But he's not one to stay outside and direct the proceedings, not our Max; he's a rowdy, likes his work, and leads the way. I say he's a lovely old bastard. He keeps us trained and sharp and any man on our team can handle any task, so he never has to stand around with the crowd getting us organized and looking official. The two of us usually bust right in and go to work, then, each careful to watch out for the other. He's sixty years old, fearless, and thinks I ought to be the next captain—though, of course, that's politics as even he knows and some dreamer like me who wants to live right in the fire station doesn't have much chance.

This alarm is another dilly: an empty apartment on the second floor of a new four-floor complex has smoldered for days with its occupants gone. It has finally erupted and the entire floor crawls with flame. We attack its fringes with water as I begin to bust doors looking for occupants. My eyes are wide with excitement because I expect anyone behind the very next door: some relative, a clerk from the grocery store where I trade, perhaps a forgotten acquaintance. Everyone I ever knew is burning up, I tell you, and my throat is tight with every new room and corridor. "Here! Over here, Coker, baby!" the captain booms, and we follow the smoke looking for its source. Fire is a tricky viper: it runs in the walls, gets in the conduits and vents, strikes at unexpected moments. I charge through a room, send an end table flying, jerk a closet open. Nothing. The snorkel passes the window, Charlie Wickers peering inside like an idiot. He never knows where he's going. We cross the hall and quickly batter through another door; these new apartment houses are like kindling, but the doors are easy to bust. As Max turns the hose on the ceiling of the hallway, I hear a cry. The walls all around us are hot and scorched, but we press on; somewhere behind all this smoke is a fist of fire we have to find—and probably a tenant or two, for I think I hear the cry again.

Rafferty arrives with another hose and coupling, so that Max directs him to retrace our steps and gather what we've trailed behind us. This keeps him busy and out of our way. We run through another series of rooms, smashing windows as we go, for the smoke thickens. A dead pussy cat, choked and gone. Water cascades helplessly against the outside of the building now, so that Max turns to me with a smirk, once, and says, "Jesus, they need to get in here where the fun is, right?" At about this point we meet a wall of heat: a kitchen, the source. Max lays down a steady stream from the hose while I quickly circle back into the hall to look for another entrance.

An old man wanders the hallway. Coughing and gagging, he grabs my arms as I hold him and we recognize each other. In the smoke he manages to speak my name, then gasps, "My daughter, in there!" And I point him on his way, assuring him there's no trouble in that direction, while I go in further search. My mother's former pastor, I knew him well: Rooker, his name was. The steepled Congregational church in Evanston. But now a variation of the dream: she is a lanky, naked girl, screaming her head off, and I can't be sure if its because of the fire or because her closet filled with clothes writhes with flames; I try to wrestle her to the window, but she fights me as if I wanted to throw her out. Reasoning with her, I see her try to cover her parts; she runs here, there, like a dazed antelope. "Quit it, please," I address her, trying to sound logical. "Just stop this and follow me out!" We wrestle again, fall, and her eyes open with even wider terror at my minor disfigurement. "Look, miss," I plead, "never mind your state. Take a blanket off the bed. Here, take it." But she claws at me, tussles free, and locks herself inside the bathroom before I can catch her again. By now the wallpaper is a sagging black curl. She screams and screams from behind that door and I pause, ax ready, and call to her. "Don't resist me, lady, come on! Wrap yourself in a towel because we don't have much time!" Her scream, then, alters into a baleful moan. Too late I dislodge the door with a single stroke. The room has caved in, and she is gone to the lapping heat; the intensity turns me away, so that I find myself in the hallway, Max's voice nearby. He has discovered the old pastor, who took a wrong turn immediately after leaving me, burned into a crisp pudding. Left for a moment to hold the hose and direct the stream of water, I recall the brief sensation of that girl's breasts on me; my thoughts flare and my whole life dances in the smoke and surging orange before me.

At the station Max and I take each other's Polaroid snapshot. He poses beside one of the pump trucks, the words *American LaFrance* beside his jutting jaw. I pose in his office beneath the only wall decoration in the station, an engraving of one of the old rigs with six plump firehorses, the good side of my face turned toward the camera.

Max knows a bit of what goes on with me, but doesn't ask much.

"You have to keep your pleasure to yourself in this business," he tells me solemnly, so I suspect he has a glimmer of what is happening. And of course he knows my bad luck these last weeks, all those near rescues and disasters, but he considers that I'm one of the bravest firemen he has ever known, someone who will match him step by step into the center of a blaze, and figures that all the victims were doomed anyway.

Perhaps he feels something more: that all the unusual number and kinds of alarms in our district have to do with me. But he keeps this to himself, for he's a man who likes to do battle.

We've been close, a team, telling each other our lives. He attended DePaul University long ago on a voice scholarship; now he is married, has a grown son, and doesn't go home when he can stay on call. He'll get up from the breakfast table or out of bed late at night and rush to help us, and he says it's for the extra money, but I know him too well. In his heart is nothing except a fire fighter. Meanwhile, I share a few vignettes of myself with him. Not a very happy childhood, but okay now. This birthmark on my left side covers my ear, my cheek, neck, and encircles my eye, and it looks something like a burn—even the skin wrinkles a bit on that side like an ill-fitting mask—and my dumb mother said this was God's kiss. My less theological schoolmates turned their eyes away, pretty girls of my dreams like popular Alice Durning of the ninth grade fretted when I came near, and even now those who give me a few necessary services—waitresses, the butcher—learn to do so without looking at me. Otherwise, until lately, I'm terribly normal; I like steak and potatoes, the Cubs, movies, and girlie magazines. Last year I read mostly the *Tribune* and *Newsweek*. I weigh one-eighty and have a few dental problems.

This is one of my sleepless nights again, so I go down to the refrigerator to cut a slice of my new cheddar and there is Max watching the late show. Glad to see him, I sit down and catch Brian Donlevy and Preston Foster in World War II. Then we talk. He's sleeping at the station because his wife's sister has arrived to occupy his bedroom. We discuss the woes of marriage, Leo Durocher, Ron Santo, slumps, bad seasons, hard luck, and getting tickets from mean cops in about that order. Max, pointing a finger, says, "Policemen need guys to break the goddamn laws, you see, just like teachers need stupid students, doctors need the sick and dying, and soldiers need victims. It's all the same."

We ponder this together and talk on.

"You know this Rooker girl?" he finally asks me.

"Knew her father," I sigh. "Or rather my mother knew him. Maybe I knew the daughter, too, a long time ago when she was just a little girl."

Max doesn't press further. He is in the presence of mystery, knows it, and prefers to let well enough alone; also, he's thinking that if the alarms go tonight he'll get in on the action.

"These girls," I muse. "We're having more and more contact, but I still don't get them out. I got scratches wrestling with this last one."

"I know, kid, I know," he comforts me. "Take it easy on yourself."

A routine day passes: two grass fires, a smoking trash dump, an auto blaze, a call for us to come wash gasoline off an intersection after an accident. Nervous, I stay at the station and don't attend these minor calls. I varnish a ladder, check couplings, show two kids around, and work a crossword puzzle. Max appears for regular duty in the afternoon and brings me a milk shake.

On the following noon we have another big one: the furnace at Parkside High School explodes and the old firetrap is a sudden maze of smoke and flame. We're the first there, Max leading the way, but the noise of every unit in The Loop is just behind us. I'm pulling on my jacket, barking at Rafferty to set up the rescue unit because the lawn is already strewn with kids crying with burns; some old biddy in a charred dress wanders among us giving off a descant of hysteria, and Wickers, the idiot, tries to ask directions of her; Max and I decide to hit the basement, where the flames are a steady roar. As we head down the concrete stairs with the hose, students trapped on the second floor call for us. "Hold on," Max promises. "Others coming!" And ladders and nets are unloaded from arriving engines as we head down toward the boiler room.

No secret where the blaze is centered this time: the boiler room heat is impossible. Max stations himself outside the door and shielded by a thin hot wall aims the hose around the corner at the flames; I try to assist, but I'm useless. "Check that far door!" he yells, so I dash by the flaming door and follow a narrow hall to a door, mostly wired glass, which I demolish. Inside, protected from the boiler room by a thick fire wall, I find no trouble, so decide to circle behind the fire. Dangerous—because Max is occupied and out of sight—but there may be someone trapped there. Anyway, I figure that the fire has spiraled upward through the blown-out ceiling and except for the furnace area the basement is possibly safe, so I bust another bolted door.

I run headlong into the locker room of the girl's gymnasium.

Madhouse: twenty or thirty girls running amok, shrieking, flitting near the flames on the side of the room where I enter, then retreating like moths. The broken door lets in a swish of oxygen and the flames suck toward it, cutting off the way I've come in as a possible exit, but I have my ax and don't panic. I go to the opposite wall, scramble over benches, climb a locker, and smash two paneled windows. "Here! Girls!"

I shout, but all movement blurs into a strange slow motion now, the room igniting in a soft and frenzied dance; the girl in white panties is Midge Prinz, I remember her well, and she glides near and brushes me. Seconds, mere seconds, I tell myself, and we're all lost, but the reel of my senses rattles and slows, everything awhirl, and here are my teachers and all the darlings of my twelfth school year—ones who refused me at the prom, others who, casting down their eyes, knew me only as a voice. The typing instructor I adored: Miss Cates. A glistening nakedness now in the scorching heat of the room, her breasts rise in a high bounce as she floats by; the same silvered fingernails, the same mouth, and she hasn't aged in all these years. (She sat cross-legged on the desk beating time on her pretty white palm with a ruler: our lovely metronome.) And I'm calling "Get out, Miss Cates, get out everyone," and my coat is off as I help one mount the locker; she slips—my gloves are gone, too—and her body wets my hands, and she grabs my neck as we fall. Midge jumps on me and rides me, her eyes rolled back, mouth agape, and pleads to hide in my arms; the far wall begins to cave in. My suspenders off my shoulders, shirt open, I toss them toward the window, but they're like dry leaves floating in the room's hot pressure; they settle against me, delirious, and a scalding kiss finds my neck. Another burns my stomach. A willowy coed circles the room with my ax, then expires; here is Miss Donnelly, too, my old homeroom teacher who taught me verses I was never allowed to recite before the class, her cotton undies in her withered grip. One girl is out, perhaps two, but the window clogs with a soft and undulating mass. Reaching up, I try to pull some of them back, but their bodies are slick with perspiration and blood where they've nicked themselves on the uneven broken glass and down we go, swooning and falling, three or four of us, and I see that my coveralls are mostly burned away, black and shredded on me, though I feel no pain. "Here!" I call again, pointing the way, but Miss Cates tackles me and over we go, my head thumping against a bench.

Then I'm outside on the cool grass. Max is there, his hands burned from holding the hose around the boiler-room door too long, and we receive treatment from two attendants. "Good work, Coke, baby," he tells me. "Just great. How you ever got out of there I'll never know."

The fire marshal visits the station, commends Max and me, but mostly talks about the increased alarms in our district. He mentions possible arson and even before he's finished his speech we're out on another call—sure enough, some joker who tries to torch his own apartment.

Back at the station later I rub salve on my neck and stomach burns and read newspaper accounts of the high-school blaze; I have to find out if I dreamed it, but here it is: two janitors dead in the initial explosion, sixteen girls and two instructors in the fateful locker room, another teacher upstairs, twenty-two on the critical list in the hospital. And here: Miss Cates and Miss Donnelly and Midge Prinz, the names just right. A fever of puzzlement comes over me.

The next morning Max arrives at the station for breakfast and we linger at coffee, whispering to each other.

"These girls," he says. "All the ones you say you recall."

"What about them?"

"Maybe they're after you, trying to keep you inside until you get burned up." His face is drawn and serious and he places a bandaged hand across my arm.

"I've thought of everything," I whisper. "You ever heard of poltergeists? People who make things fly through the air or who move objects with their thoughts?"

"Could be," he answers, his jaw set. Good old Max.

"I've wondered if some corner of my brain is setting fire to things. But there's more I don't understand. Miss Cates, for example. God, how could she be in that school?"

"I know this," Max adds. "We've never had such a season for alarms. And one of the nation's biggest, too, right here in our district."

"Someone could be playing a joke on me, but I know that isn't it," I muse, my coffee going cold in my hands. "And it isn't a dream either—I know that much because of the newspapers."

Max pats my arm again and gives me a look of wonder and sympathy.

"Let's not worry about it," he concludes. "We both know something big is coming, another alarm. We feel it, right?"

"You too, eh?"

"Oh, sure, Coker, god, you think I don't feel it? My knees get weak. I know something else is coming."

Waiting, now, Max keeps me at the station during all small alarms. I set all the equipment in order: the asbestos suits, the Pyrene foam, the new soap machine, the "wet water" and other smothering agents. I dream of sophisticated disasters—all sorts of mean chemical fires and special catastrophes.

I speculate, also, on my peculiar malady; is it part of what's happening in the city, I wonder, and the whole crazy world? Is it anarchy breaking loose? The overthrow of reason by dark forces? Such involved speculations annoy me. I'm a simple case, I assure myself: a regular guy, somewhat marred, but on balance; I had some rough adolescent moments, sure, but shook them off. I wish none of these victims ill will, never did; I do my duty, think baseball and hamburgers, take pride in being Max's partner.

Why, though, why?

Somewhere, I know, a match has fallen into a chair to smolder; rags are seething into combustion in some stuffy closet; a cigarette has fallen away from someone's sleeping fingers, and my answer is out there.

On the day I begin to understand, I'm busy repairing the spring on a hose reel. Max and I have exchanged glances all morning and the afternoon has worn away into twilight. The reel is a bitch to fix, but I'm grateful for the preoccupation and my tools are spread out in the office so that I can monitor the phones and the flashboard which lights when one of the sprinkler systems in our district is set off by heat.

The bell, when it finally comes, causes me to drop a wrench. Even before I finish taking information on the call, Max comes down the pole, bandages and all, and starts up number one truck.

Another explosion: this time in the lab of the big clinic over near Seward Park.

Seconds now: our rhythms are quick, practiced, and no squad in the city is better. We're halfway there in sixty seconds, and I think of the job, a lab explosion: chemical, perhaps, after all, so I strap on a portable extinguisher filled with foam.

Outside the building, a large rambling affair of only two floors, Max neatly dispatches the troops; the problem is clearly to save lives and evacuate the hospital wing. We confer in an instant with a young doctor who shouts information about the floor plan, then off we go. Always helter-skelter in spite of briefings, we move into infernos never really knowing where things are. Just another job hazard.

Most of our men head toward the wards to aid the patients, but Max, an edge on his voice, calls for me to join him down near the blaze, where someone may be trapped. So we start down another hallway toward what seems a holocaust, though there isn't much smoke because great holes have been blown in the sides of the lab; the flame boils, then, and the heat turns us inside a room.

We stand in there panting, Max saying, "That hallway is hell. Let's check out the rooms down here real quick and not get caught out there." I nod, reach back, touch my foam gun to make sure.

Then we rush out, each of us taking one side of the hallway. My first room, an office, yields no one, so I move to the second. A small examination room, nothing again, though it has a door which leads into the next. The windows are gone, I notice, and medicines and instruments are scattered: all signs of a whopping blast. And what happens next takes only seconds, another instant frozen in that old slow motion as I perceive it— for all our work is such, a science played against the clock and one's personal daring. As I pass through the door another explosion buckles the walls and I feel the hot gush of fire at my back; hurled forward into the room, everything yellow and searing, I see a woman, a nurse, as we're enveloped. Death has its hot instant, but I have some reflexes left; we're together in the far corner beside a metal table, crouched low, fire spewing through the broken walls as I open my foam gun to fight the flames head on. The heat drives the substance back around us and suddenly we are in a cocoon of foam, a soft sponge of protection, and my eyes close, and I'm away, dreamlike, letting go.

A floating bed of airy whiteness: in its liquid folds her limbs entwine me and her body opens. We heave and settle together in the old slow dance, cushioned in rapture, and the flames are distant things, painless, as she receives me. The gun empties, my finger relaxes on the trigger, and I'm gone, my senses incandescent. Lips and legs and a glowing thrust of skin: she bakes with me, melts, while the foam holds and caresses us. Then we lie still as the room subsides.

It is Rafferty, brave soul, who comes and plucks me out.

Strange, how suddenly doom and deliverance occur; we rush in, spurt water and bust doors in what seems a comic dream, take our consequences. Fate is a moment, a mere puff.

I insist, later, on leaving the rescue unit where they've bedded me down; stepping down from the van into the street, my legs wobbly, I view the carnage. Half the building is collapsed, thousands of gallons of water are still being pumped, and the pavement is lined with stretchers. I stroll among them, doped slightly from something they've given me, checking myself; I'm a mess—second-degree burns on my back and forehead. Shouts and sirens punctuate the scene, but I don't pay attention.

They show me poor Max, who really isn't there anymore. Then I go over and look at the nurse; the attendant pulls back the sheet and there she is, calm, the little black nameplate intact on her white uniform: ALICE DURNING. I lift my eyes back to the tower of smoke which moves across the early night.

What's happening to me, what?

I wander for another hour before someone leads me back to shelter.

On the way to the hospital, I have a curious surge of

elation; I think, well, I'm alive, I made it again, and I'll be patched up soon enough and back listening for alarms. It's going to be exciting—and they might give me a chance at captain, so I'll always go in first. I'll be a lot like Max in that way. Then, moments later, depression sets in; my obsession waylays me again, and I think, what's wrong with me? I'm kissed by a strange and awful God; my dread and my desire are one.

The Good Ship Erasmus

This is one of those cruise ships dedicated to helping people. These ships embark every day now from all over the world, some of them stuffed with psychiatrists trying to help the passengers forget their troubles, others with physical-culture experts trying to beat the blubber off a fat clientele, others with religious leaders trying to purge or mystify those who are aboard.

Our ship, the *Erasmus*, has a somewhat less complicated mission: theoretically, at least, it is just a ship which will hold us captive on the high seas until we have all stopped smoking. We sailed from Amsterdam a few days ago, puffing like mad on the dock before the horn sounded, and in a few short weeks we will be around Italy, the warm Mediterranean waters soothing us—one hope being, I assume, that craved minds will turn away from nicotine to romantic lust—until all lungs are healthy again.

My game is smuggling thousands of cigars and cigarettes on board.

By the time we see the French coast I'm largely in control of many of the three hundred lives around me.

It is enough to make me slightly melancholy, philosophic. I stand here at the rail gazing into the calm summer waves, ruminating on the nature of evil.

The *Erasmus* has twin stabilizers, a cruising speed of twenty-six knots, lounges, shops, bars, a gymnasium, swimming pools, dining rooms, and an optimistic staff. Perry Cheyenne is the Passenger Host who directs our seminars, offers encouragement to those in withdrawal and despair, arranges parties and games and contests. He wears tennis clothes and a yacht cap, grins, bounces as he goes. Our captain is never seen, just this happy Passenger Host. The captain is far away, up there somewhere on the bridge, steering us onward.

Shopping for clothes, I buy tennis wear just like Perry's and give serious consideration to a maroon tuxedo. I boarded with four oversized suitcases and a trunk all stuffed with everyone's favorite brands, domestic and foreign, so had only my one business suit.

I do all this because of the character of our age. It grows difficult to find a situation in which one can be clearly immoral, in which one can be sure of his wicked deeds.

"I'd *give* you the tux, mister, for one lousy cigarette, believe me," sighs Ramona, the salesgirl. She is working her passage on this expensive cruise here in the men's shop.

"I have plenty of cigarettes in my cabin," I disclose, admiring the cut of the jacket.

She eyes me wantonly.

"What price you asking?" she blurts out, incapable of coyness.

"There are many prices," I tell her. "The cost isn't always the same."

* * *

The Good Ship Erasmus

There are deeper elements in all this beyond the fact of its being a simple tobacco-curing sea voyage. There is the death of God, the tides of history, my own somewhat complicated personality. It's very confusing, sorting it out, which accounts for the choppy style of this report. Also, not only do I lose track of the exact philosophic flow, but my attention span, like yours, is short.

On deck, naturally, we passengers exchange personal information.

My father was from Chicago, my mother from Geneva, and I was born in the skiing village of Igls above Innsbruck as an American citizen. Father was an author and consumer of thick books and in his library I spent my asthmatic adolescence, ducking out of boarding schools to sit among his volumes instead. Once, six days into my puberty—I knew you'd want this incidental and inevitable note—I seduced our young Austrian housekeeper. I traveled and studied. Soon I knew many things and some of these which I tell my fellow passengers are:

The earliest cavemen lived in caves on the French Riviera very near the beach and sunshine.

The poet Rilke died from being pricked by a rose thorn.

The population of the world now doubles every thirty years.

Scheherazade's erotic *Thousand and One Nights* ends with a prayer.

The only place to get a drink on Sunday morning in Rome is inside the bar at St. Peter's.

Choose one.

Sitting in deck chairs together, Mrs. Murtaugh and I discuss our separate problems. She is already beginning to resist therapy and sits here sucking a dummy cigarette, a little wooden Tinker Toy.

"My seminar group is meeting right now," she wails, "but I just can't go today. I don't like my hypnotist. If you don't respond to your hypnotist, he just can't put you under so you might as well quit."

"This is a degrading sort of troublemaking," I complain, "coming on board a sailing vessel and peddling smokes. In another age I might've been a satanic figure, my life a tragedy of corruption. Now look at me: I go around letting those of weak wills sniff the nicotine on my fingers and smell my brown breath."

"Worse yet," she continues, "I can't make love without a ciggie. I *have* to catch a smoke before and afterwards or I just can't go for sex. I told my group leader that and I told that insensitive hypnotist, too!"

"The world is too libertine," I muse aloud. "In another age I could've been Iago, but not now. I take the whole reckless curse of human history back to its cosmic roots, too, and the lost sense of the divine."

"So here I sit in a dowdy deck chair! A deck chair! I'm only fifty-six years old! I'm a warm-blooded woman, let me *tell* you, and a cruise is a cruise!"

"One could blame God, of course, for making man finite. A really benevolent God would've made man his equal—been a sport about the creation, I mean—but no, man is a weak hybrid, lower than the angels. And so it was certain to come to this: a time when the moral distinctions completely blur. Man adrift in a sensual sea. Perfecting the rhythms of pandemonium."

"What'd you say you peddled? Did you say ciggies?"

"I once wanted to be really evil. For instance, I thought of things like murder. But the whole world has too strong a death drive on its own—nothing very original can be done even with murder! And sex criminals can't get a headline because their perversions are so everyday. I spent my teen years practicing lots of nasty habits, I mean, but now there're movies and songs celebrating these things! I'm trying to get across the point, Mrs. Murtaugh, that all my life I've dreamt about doing people in, but fortune has only left me a few petty hustles."

"Did you say you actually have ciggies?"

Clearly, Mrs. Murtaugh isn't quite on my frequency as I describe the final indifference of the Greeks to their gods, Dante's rejection of religion in favor of secular politics, the Renaissance, growth of the factories, Einstein. Her eyes fasten on me as I talk and gaze out toward the Spanish coast, but she hears little.

At last, yes, I say, yes, Mrs. Murtaugh, I'll take your BankAmericard.

Everyone scampers ashore at Bilbao, the Bay of Biscay glistening in the hot sun around the *Erasmus* as I wait on board. By this time those who have resisted me run boldly toward the nearest cafés where they pay outlandish prices for packs of Pipers, Celtas, and other mediocre Spanish cigarettes.

Perry stands astride the gangplank, meanwhile, with his good-natured shakedown crew. When passengers return with bulges under their sport shirts and Bermuda shorts, the crew searches them and laughingly tosses their goodies into the bay. I look on with approval. A mere twenty dollar bribe passed my contraband aboard without the slightest inspection and I disdain the lack of foresight and these clumsy attempts on the lone returning gangplank.

Perry gives the fallen few pep talks, making a fist as

he lectures like a determined prep-school coach. Both his teeth and shoes glisten white.

Two of my customers are caught smoking in one of the cramped hatches and Perry and his crew suffer doubts over their effectiveness at the gangplank. Perry shames the offenders in front of a Combined Seminar Meeting in the auditorium, shredding their cigarettes in public. One of them, a civic leader from Palatine, Illinois, nearly weeps. I respect Perry's zeal.

After this spectacle there is a speech by the ship's doctor, who says things like, "Please, *folks,* don't poison your body!" Then we have a demonstration by the hypnotist whose victim is a long-legged girl named Daphne. When she swoons many in the audience are visibly moved.

There aren't enough chairs and the room is crowded, so I move among the throng like a savage force. Here and there I catch a knowing eye.

The famous Danish porno cruise ship, *Flicka,* passes us after we turn back into the Atlantic. Dedicated to orgy-minded travelers, it flies a single red flag and moves by us slowly on the hint of music.

Erasmus lists to port as we pass, my envious fellow passengers out there clutching the rail for a good look. Soon it is beyond our wake.

Pensive, my philosophical mood hanging on, yet talkative, I consent to my assigned session with one of the psychiatrists-in-residence, a Doctor Gonatt. He is impressed by my Austrian background and remarks that he once tried to read one of Father's novels.

Gonatt strives to comprehend me and suggests an arrested moral growth brought on by culture fatigue, and

I have some difficulty explaining, no, I am actually an advanced and complex monster and that dedication to evil usually has curious and subtle side benefits for mankind anyway. We all know the evil that good men invariably do, I point out, but we must also consider the ironic value of the deviate. The sheep is not truly itself without the wolf, I explain, fetching an illusion which escapes him.

We talk and talk.

Gonatt has a drinking problem, I learn, and is trying to recover financially so he can reopen his clinic near San Diego. He used to smoke a pipe, he recalls: a big, curve-stemmed meerschaum with a bowl like a factory chimney.

As he prattles his hands begin to tremble, so I can do no other than offer a menthol filter which, naturally, he accepts.

Here I sit in the Desiderius Bar, the ship's plushest lounge, with the keys to my closet and locker safely rattling in my pocket, content that the stewards who clean my cabin will never find anything, but one of my best customers comes over and informs me that Perry Cheyenne is onto somebody. Paranoid, I consider returning to B Deck and checking my hoard, but I calm myself.

"Watch your step, pal," my customer advises. His name is Mr. Branch, a successful food expert from Brussels, and he has never indulged in such side-of-the-mouth dramatics before.

I offer the next barstool. "Steady now. Tell me what's happening," I say evenly, trying to reassure him.

He insists there are high-level meetings involving Perry, the captain, the ship's doctor, and certain spies. Perry is furious. There have been butts in the public rooms and telltale holes burned in a few of the bed linens.

I buy poor Branch a drink and promise an extra pack for his loyalty, but inside me I feel a stirring: a tingle of excitement, a new pulse. Deep down, perhaps, I crave a confrontation.

I wear my maroon tuxedo to the evening dance. I know that Perry watches me as I make the rounds talking and laughing. The game seems to be on.

Later, back in my cabin I can't sleep. I know that a showdown with Perry might be inevitable, yet it isn't what I want. Specifically, I need an intellectual adversary—not just some giddy zealot.

The captain: one wonders what or who he is.

Beyond Gibralter the nights turn suddenly hot and life on the *Erasmus* grows intense. Pairing off seems to occupy everybody's time and the ship begins to rock with new diversions. Girls in bikinis, laughing, spring from one deck to another; the men are brown and strangely healthy in spite of my booming business, their coughs lessened, and all the meals and games are attacked with gusto.

At the pool there is hardly room for me to splash around. One of the major lounges has been converted into a lively casino, games in every corner, and the Desiderius is packed with roaring drunks.

Perry seems content that such revelry excludes smoking, but a few of us detect his almost imperceptible discontent. Perhaps the slant of his yacht cap. A bounce slightly lessened.

However, before the floor show and dance he leads us in our nightly deep-breathing exercises, slapping his hands loudly and giving off his familiar "Hey, everybody, now!"

Afterward the usual crowd of female enthusiasts are around him, gushing, admiring his stamina.

Out on deck I stroll along moodily until my shopgirl, Ramona, comes and takes my arm. I speak of the ancient Roman mentality which resulted in Nero, the acute aesthetic awareness of certain high Nazis, the occasional meditations of De Sade which, in my opinion, soared beyond his more frequent banality.

Meanwhile, Ramona nuzzles my neck.

From high on the bridge comes a green glow from the captain's window.

The sea is moderate.

Mrs. Murtaugh and Dr. Gonatt pass by holding hands.

We anchor offshore at Cannes. Everyone pours down into the awaiting launches to go ashore and visit the film festival, shop, strut around the promenade, and of course steal a few drags.

Near the beach just outside the Hotel Martinez photographers encircle a movie starlet who tries to contain herself in a peekaboo swimsuit. As I linger near this confusion, my thoughts momentarily meandering on to the nature of publicity and its role in the world's present corruption, I find Perry beside me. He makes a tsk-tsk at the proceedings, appears friendly, but I take this seemingly accidental appearance as ominous.

"How's everything going?" I query him.

"Not awfully well," he admits. "We should have many more passengers cured by now than we do."

"Oh? How many do we have?"

"At last night's staff meeting we estimated fifteen percent—far below normal. I've been ramrod on cruises where we got fifty percent."

Now I make a tsk-tsk.

We exchange a few minutes of small talk there on the promenade until the starlet backpedals into the hotel with her fixed smile. Then Perry excuses himself and ambles away and, yes, I see that his bouncy walk has modified.

No doubt of it: he's worried and this banter was an ill omen. Why me?

In the cover of darkness, later, I transfer my diminished stock into the locked cabinets beneath the hand-painted ties and initialed handkerchiefs in Ramona's men's shop. For a mere pack a day, she is now my dealer and accomplice and it's none too soon.

Sicily is admired for its lovely cliffs above the sea, its hearty peasants, its wines, but I admire it for its history of violence.

As we pass by on a sunny noon, I cease whittling my Christian name into the rail and salute with my pocket-knife.

The captain asks to see me.

When Perry presents himself at my cabin door with this message I feel excitement. Do they have evidence, I wonder, or are they bluffing? Will the captain be a worthy adversary? Even if I'm caught dead to rights with Ramona as the unshakable witness for the prosecution, what could they possibly do to me?

I dress slowly in my all-whites. Take, I caution myself, every possible psychological advantage. My thoughts spin like dervishes.

They're just no match for me, neither Perry nor his eager scouts. Also, I've committed no crime and at most they can only put me ashore at one of these lovely southern ports. And what could they possibly say? I'm intellectually stockpiled to parry their pious thrusts.

The Good Ship Erasmus

Perry waits smugly for me in the corridor and escorts me up to Deck AA. Every step I'm practicing my argument.

Society has gone mad, so that as the man of reason tries to apply his reason to madness he is being absurd. He thinks he is doing good as he uses his wit against the world's puzzle, I'll tell them, but he's actually trying to ponder the unfathomable. Not only is he a useless dolt, but he's even harmful because he misleads others. The true monster, however: ah, he goes his wicked way, attracts constant notoriety, and possibly teaches mankind a hard lesson in morality—in spite of himself.

We reach Deck AA. A long walk to the bridge.

My lips move as I practice my lines.

Perry, straight of back, knocks with authority on the door, opens it, and ushers me inside. Before us is the helm of the ship—a big wheel just like in swashbuckling movies—and the luminous green eye of a large compass. The walls are dingy white and beyond the wide, salt-sprayed windows the bow breaks the waves.

The captain isn't present.

Nervously, Perry announces that we should wait.

As we stand in silence I take a good look at the bridge. It seems vaguely familiar—although I've never been in such a place before—yet also personalized and different. The captain, wherever he is, is clearly a man of reading habits; paperbacks, a few antiquated leather-bound volumes, magazines and newspapers are stuffed into the shelves behind the desk. There is also a narrow, uncomfortable-looking bed.

When I inquire, Perry admits that sometimes the old man sleeps up here and doesn't bother to go below.

A variety of clothing is strewn around. Not a very neat man, I surmise, and I count two frayed naval topcoats, a rain slicker, a few discolored turtlenecks, underwear, socks, and, curiously enough, a shawl.

Perry shows his discomfort as I observe all this.

Soon there is a whistle, a cough, and another whistle from an instrument near the compass and Perry dashes over there. A man from the boiler room—I can hear, in the midst of his profanities, talks of gaskets and seals—says that the captain is down there, grease up to the elbows, yes, dammit, and, no, there's nothing seriously wrong, but the captain can't make it. I'm to come back later, the voice says, because the captain has the opinion that the appointment isn't urgent.

This frustrates us. Primed for accusation and argument, I start to protest. Perry, his smugness gone, sputters and asks if he shouldn't remain and steer the ship, but the voice answers hell no, naturally not, the ship's locked on course.

Embarrassed, Perry says he must attend to his many duties and offers that I'll have to find my own way to see the captain.

"No problem," I say. "Get on with your business."

He's visibly shaken. His yacht cap sags as he tells me that Deck AA is often closed to passengers, that I should probably seek written permission, that, er, perhaps another crew member could escort me.

"You heard the man in the boiler room," I answer. "It's nothing big. I'll stop around again when it's convenient for everyone."

The cigarettes are untouched, safely there underneath the counter in Ramona's shop. She doesn't understand why I kiss her cheek.

Later, alone, I probe the aspects of my new advantage. Either they were bluffing or they have the barest suspicion. At any rate, now I'm free to make this a real

The Good Ship Erasmus

intellectual rendezvous, a true confrontation; I'll bring down the weight of Nietzsche, Machiavelli, and all the obscure Mongol thinkers on that innocent captain's arguments.

The best time to catch the old sea dog, I reason, will be in the evening, so I wait until the day's seminars finish and the dances begin before making my way to the bridge once more.

Empty. The ship is still automatically fixed on course. I peer through the window at the green glow of the compass. Eerie.

Feeling odd, I go back to my cabin, slip into my maroon tuxedo, and take refuge in the music of the Desiderius.

The next day I make frequent trips up to Deck AA, but the old boy is never there.

On one of my visits I try the door and find it open. Inside, I casually grip the wheel. On the nearby desk are charts—an outline of the Italian coast around Amalfi. I exchange stares with the omnipotent compass, gaze off at the horizon where, dimly, far away to port, lies the coast.

The wheel, yes, is fixed on course. Comforting.

Days pass.

Perry is deep in a frenzy of work now, seemingly having forgotten me. The seminars are booming therapy sessions with the members shouting obscenities at each other, vomiting up their private lives, accusing and demanding, and Perry is there, I learn, orchestrating all of it. When I see him on deck his clothes are soiled and wrinkled, his hair is long and hanging from his yacht cap, his eyes weary.

I hear of a bloody fight in the casino lounge.

Beside the nearly empty swimming pool—one fat man lolling on his back—I take a glum stroll. After a while I sit down on the tile, deciding not to take my swim.

Where, I wonder, is our elusive captain?

Tonight after checking the bridge again I visit the boiler room, but the engines are purring unattended. There seems to be no one above or below, just Perry and his bedraggled crew working amidships with an increasingly restless cargo of passengers. The voyage is too long for us, I tell myself.

Toward morning I wander back toward the vacant bridge. Prying, I rummage around in the captain's desk —paper clips, parchments, a service medal, the passenger list, a quill pen—and pull a few books off the shelves. A few first editions nobody would ever read. Magazines: popular European gossip items, nudist-camp publications, occult periodicals, journals on sports, wildlife, travel, cuisine.

And who is my eclectic adversary? An ordinary escapist, the Flying Dutchman, some alienated intelligence, just a shy and simple pilot?

Before departing again, I trace my finger over the charts. Not too difficult reading charts, I conclude; the deeps and shallows are clearly marked.

The scent of the Greek isles rides the wind.

At times, now, I forget exactly where we're putting into final port.

My mind is on last diversions—parties, another amateur night, my shopgirl who insists she has fallen in love with me, testimonials in the Desiderius for those few who have actually kicked the habit—and I am still playing hide-and-seek with the old sea wolf upstairs.

Disheveled, a mere wisp of a smile left on his face,

Perry goes around patting everyone on the back and making the best of a cruise low on converts.

A few brave passengers grin sheepishly, shrug, and light up the last of my dwindling supply in public.

On the bridge again.

Once more I take a grip on the helm and peer out over the bow, but this time I'm surprised to find that we're not on a fixed course and that I'm alone at the wheel. The locking device: yes, here it is. I see, it must be part of an automatic system with the compass. Sure.

The compass illuminates the darkened room in a cozy green glow, my charts curl, and I slip into one of the turtlenecks.

Long days and nights.

Far out now, no sign of land.

We have a westerly course, a good barometer.

The new Passenger Host pops in, salutes, makes happy small talk, and reports that the new passengers are settled into seminars. His name is, I think, Jerry, and he asks if I'll have my meals up here today and I say, yes, please. I watch him bounce away in his whites, calling and waving to someone below as he descends.

Later he returns with a crisp new passenger list, the mimeograph ink hardly dry. I read over it wondering if any of these passengers might be capable of philosophical discussion.

My Ramona is gone.

We made a stop somewhere, exchanged everyone, took on supplies, set forth again, and the most curious thing about this is that my new quarters are filled with cigarettes.

Under the House

His name is Johnny Breck, plumber: that much is lettered on the side of his service truck. For years he has unstopped toilets, fitted pipes, seduced housewives, and lived a single obsession: he will not, no matter what, go under the house.

He awakes, as usual, alone in the clutter of his shop: copper tubing, elbows and joints, washers and tools surround him, and on his walls old yellowed Petty Girl pin-ups (his father's relics) and some new spread-eagled porno. He fumbles toward his coffeepot, glances at the schedule on his clipboard, sighs, and begins his day. The face in the washbasin mirror is the same handsome face with dark eyes and hair and stubble—and the ever-present drool: that thin viper of saliva which forms in the corner of his lips as though some deep inner pipe has a pinhole leak. He shaves and thinks of Wendie as the drool wedges out a small path in the lather of his chin.

A bleak rainy day. In his truck he rattles toward Wendie's apartment house, passing places he knows too well. Other jobs await him and he doesn't altogether want to go back to that house just now, but Wendie and the other girls draw him there.

This is a small college town not far from St. Louis and his only competitors are the Marston Brothers, Plumbing Contractors, with their fleet of trucks and fancy uniformed staff. Johnny has been here sixteen years—he can't believe it, thinking back—and gets business from the college kids and tumbledown parts of town because he works cheaper. Of course he offends some and has twice been reported, but the housewives and girls favor him as often as not. It used to be like rape, he muses, but now it's much easier; sometimes, now, I take out the old plunger and they say, hey, okay, and don't even ask me to forget the bill afterward. And now Wendie's: sometimes he wonders if this is too much of a good thing.

"Where am I wanted today, honey?" he asks as he takes a second cup of coffee in her kitchen.

"You're wanted all over the house," she tells him, winking. "But go up to Ramona's room and fix the toilet. You couldn't get to it last week, remember? And get the laundry room today, okay?"

Wendie, the sly one. She's mostly his kind of girl, liquid in movement, thin and flowing, and she stands there this morning with her terry cloth hanging open, a brown patch of thigh exposed. She's only a young thing, half his age, a part-time student at the college, but she bought this rickety house near the campus, painted it, and filled it with strong-minded girls like herself. The girls, the girls: they're quick nowadays and they go into business, like Wendie, instead of working at part-time jobs; they bang the boys when they feel like it—which seems to be more often; they demand and instruct and one of them in this very house, once, told him just how to do it—with the wrench, please, still in hand.

"I want to see you tonight," he tells Wendie, downing the coffee, and his words are somehow wrong. One doesn't make a date with Wendie.

"Maybe," she allows. "But what I need right now are some good flushing johns and the work in the laundry room."

"I don't work underneath, I told you that," he says, and he picks up his tool chest and goes up to Ramona. The stairs creak under his weight, a sad sound, and spittle drips on his shoe as he trudges up. He wishes he hadn't mentioned his problem. This place fascinates and annoys: it flows free—as he always imagined he'd like a house of girls to do—but also spooks him. Wendie, too: as much as he appreciates her he feels a trickle of worry which she sets loose in him.

He repairs the metal arm in back of Ramona's toilet and dreams of old times. A big girl with the thick white hands of her profession, Ramona is a nurse over at Washington General Hospital and she leers at him in the old way sometimes, like a hard, bitchy, whore of a housewife, and she goes around in her bra and half-slip as if to say, always, what's in yr toolbox, buster? But he dreams, dreams; he remembers a girl, everything except her name, near this very street, and how he beat her up and kissed her neck and made her climb into his overalls with him. "We're both gonna get in these things!" he yelled at her. "Put your legs down there and we'll button up!" And she went hysterical and pounded his chest while he stuffed her inside. Or the foxy coed over on Gregg Avenue who called him to unstop her sink the morning after a big party and stood there in her negligee dragging on a cigarette until he asked her if she wasn't tired of college boys. And she said yes when he made his first moves, then no, then cried—over the torn nightwear as much as anything—and later sent two football players around to his shop. He bashed one with a two-inch pipe and the other, the bastard, just turned white. Arrested and acquitted over that little fracas.

Women: he recalls how they used to be, luring him, then retreating; teasing him, then making him break them down. All the coy sluts of yesteryear. At Wendie's apartments things are different, almost perilous.

Ramona arrives now, yawning and willing, yet asking, "My toilet, Johnny Cake: just finish it first, right?" Like Wendie and the others she is tough and practical and diminishes the excitement. Or, he allows, I might be getting older; a few years ago the old plunger never quit and I could feel the surf of my pulse with every new girl I grabbed. Is this it, age?

After the toilet he services Ramona—though not, he suspects, to her fullest satisfaction. Then he lingers. He wants to talk, but Ramona is busy dressing for her tour of duty at the hospital and Wendie calls upstairs, "You fixing the laundry room drain today? Hey, Johnny, if I'm paying you by the hour don't just sit around! Look at the drainage!" Frustrated, he trudges back downstairs.

He begs another cup of coffee from Wendie—his stomach burns already with the day's caffeine—and again mentions coming by later. She wears blue jeans now, a loose man's shirt, and glances up at him from a book the size of an encyclopedia.

"Suit yourself on that," she tells him. "But, look, we can't run this house in rainy weather unless we get the washroom straight. We're students here and career girls and the fixtures and machines have to work right, so we need you. We've got worries of our own."

"I'm *tending* to things," he snaps at her defensively, leaving her to her book. Not a trace of friendliness in her voice. A moody girl that keeps a man off guard. And as he sips, a tiny resentment builds in him, one he has often felt with Wendie: she thinks of me, he decides, as Mr. Fixit, nothing else. He determines to come back later and give her a rough toss in the sack. Later in the moondark he'll hold her so she can't get away and whisper such awful things in her ear that she'll never take him lightly again.

He takes supper in a diner.

He goes back to his shop, watches television for an hour, then turns it off and sits there in the ruins: pipes and tubing and litter of tools around him in all their forlorn dust.

His father's business before him, all this. The old man piddled in this same shop, moped and pined his weeks away because long, long years before his wife, Johnny's mother, had cut out. She had been a looker (that's where I get my beauty, no doubt of it, he considers) which left a hole in the old man's life when she went away. Jack T. Breck and Son, and the father had only Petty Girls and nightmares after that and the son —never as good a plumber, admit it—ran his hands up underneath all the skirts that came into reach. He was not one to mope and pine.

And wouldn't go under the houses, not as a little boy and not later. Yet, Johnny wishes he hadn't blabbed that again to Wendie; he doesn't like this exposed.

But what's down there? You know, you know exactly: the slow drip of water which bangs against the brain, caverns and galleries of silence, mazes of pipe. And why not go down there and fix things? Oh, because you'll never get out, not ever, and that's where the girls want you, down underneath where the terrors have to be dealt with, where the old cobwebbed limbo is.

Think of something else.

There were always three good places to break a housewife down into sex, he muses, and these were, according to the type of woman being attacked, the bathroom, the kitchen, and the laundry room. Bathrooms first and best: a woman is used to being naked in there and once the attack gets properly under way she folds easily; she doesn't want to go off to her husband's bed in the next room even if she's hot and ready, and there we are, very close, our voices magnified by the porcelain around us, and there it is, my old plunger, my fine plumber's helper, in all that cold whiteness. For another type of housewife, the kitchen: she makes me her substitute husband and pops a cookie in my mouth. We make reassuring talk, things safe, and as my fingers steal into her housecoat she is fairly calm, thinking, this is almost normal, he's a lonely bachelor without a home or the domestic cookie to aid him through the years. She resists, but her wifely ways help her to succumb and I take her. Finally, the uppity sort: the wives of guys over in the big houses on Mount Sequoia, say, or the stuck-up chicks in the fancy apartments. The laundry room for them—where all their dirty undies and gritty wash makes them see themselves for what they are and breaks them down. No way they can pretend: I pull them down around their overflowing hampers, force a kiss in those stinking clothes, make them breathe their stench and mine.

He tells all this to Wendie, hoping to make her as uncomfortable as she makes him. It is after midnight, still pouring rain, and he has returned to her apartment house and bed.

For the first time ever, he notes, she is propped on an elbow listening to him.

The apartment house is quiet, a few distant hushed voices.

"Tell me about your parents," she urges him.

Instead, he gives her more stories of his conquests. He used to go into dingy shacks, he explains, where the ghetto girls regarded plumbers as successful executives. They obeyed, whatever he told them, like slaves. And no, it wasn't exactly rape, how he dealt with them in those days; more like armed robbery than forced entry, he tells Wendie, grinning, amused at his metaphor. "I was the tough type," he says. "So they just came across. Nowadays the girls make the moves and the town is full of sensitive college boys and pansies, right?"

"Did you fight in the war?" she wants to know.

Again, he hedges. He talks about his labors in the college dorms before the Marston Brothers got the school contract.

"Did all this sex make you feel powerful? Was that it?" She sits up on the bed beside him now. She has, he senses, a curious dislike for him. But this is more emotion than ever before.

"I'll bet you drink too much, too," Wendie speculates. He grows irritated with her, reclines, puts his hands behind his head on the pillow, and thinks, ah, she doesn't understand a real man. I know *her* sort all too well, though she doesn't know me: she probably considers herself political, thinks she's a brilliant amateur psychologist, and is really interested in money and sex more than she likes to admit. And likes my style, too, if she'd admit it. He takes her arm and twists her toward him.

"This hurt?" he asks with a sneer of a grin.

"Not at all," she says. "But leggo."

He requests that she kiss the small bead of drool from his lip, but she refuses.

"Why won't you go under the house?" she asks him.

A smart ploy. A tiny rivulet of terror opens in him with that question.

"I've been underneath and don't like it," he tries to answer simply, but she reads the glint in his eyes.

"Are you afraid of spiders and rats?"

"Me?" he asks. "Are you kidding?" A small vision arrives: he sees the boy, little Johnny, riding with old Jack the Plumber years ago, and they visit a place on the outskirts of town where the storm cellar is a black mouth beside the house; or, he listens at a basement door while his father works down there in the dark with the moaning pipes; he sees himself pausing at yet another gaping slot, peering in, the dank odors rising at him.

"You got a thing about dark places, Johnny?" she goes on.

He hears his voice in denial, now, and her voice persisting, but he doesn't speak of what he knows is down there, beneath the floors and carpets where the world breaks open into vast cavities of gloom. Wendie excavates the dark places, he knows, because she wants to break me down, but no; should the plumber plumb the depths of despair? Should he ever doubt himself?

"I'm a pretty good upstairs man, that's all you need to know," he tells her. "I'm the man of the house—this or any other." And he boasts that he could service the whole house this very night; he could give all pipes a turn, he announces, and give all leaks a proper bandage, and give all residents some of the old plunger.

Wendie, more excited than he has ever seen her, twists away and throws on her terry cloth. Pointing a finger at him, she laughs, "Ha, okay: wait right here, Johnny, you wait!" And she springs from the room and down the hallway.

Suddenly he feels his tap open, his adrenalin flow, and he bounds after her, dizzy with his energy and prospects. Drool glistens, his muscles twitch with anticipation, a giddy pressure builds in his veins, and he is after her, naked, the old plunger dancing like a wild hose, and the hallway is ashriek with delight as Doris, Ramona, Wendie, and all the others whose names he can't remember bolt in view around him.

He lunges toward one, then another, and hears one scream, "Get his toolbox!" and, sure enough, all the lewd instruments of his trade are among them like toys: syringes, thick washers, spigots, gaskets. He chases one of them back to her room—who is this? Mary Sue with the raven hair?—and falls on her neck with a nasty suck before the others pull him away.

A cascade of bodies: they pour over him.

They become a pool, dragging him under, but not easily; he splashes to the surface, pumps, dives, heaves up a tidal wave of honeyed rumps as his plunger foams and over they go. The bed collapses. They become a shower, pelting him, and his hands are in their wet places as they spit and gasp. They become a river, then, bearing him off, and he is a heavy barge riding their wake as they go downstairs. Wendie takes his face in her hands and kisses him deeply, a kiss that makes a momentary whirlpool of his senses, and he tongues her back. Ramona, close enough to nibble on him, smells antiseptic. He swims, now, in the ripple of their laughter and knows deep down in the coldest undercurrents of his thoughts that he'll never see his shop again, never rattle through town in his truck, but no matter. He has opened a spring of feeling in the tough frozen ground where these bitches live. The downstairs bathtub now: they toss him inside, turn on the shower, mouth him, lather his hair, and sketch patterns on his soapy chest with their fingers. A sweet typhoon of bodies, too many: he feels, momentarily, drained and alone with them.

He manufactures a wan smile, recoups himself. "This is an orgy, a regular orgy," he says breathlessly to Wendie, and receives from her a darting glance of pity. A great soggy exhaustion begins, but he drives himself. Back in the hallway, he makes a halfhearted grab for one that gets away. Another pops her head out of a doorway and he follows; gone when he gets there. Another surfaces from a closet, so he goes there only to be distracted en route by another, leaping by in a spray of nakedness, touching him, then giggling out of sight. Squeals of laughter cheer him on—a high and musical descant everywhere. One of them, toweling herself dry from those minutes in the bathtub with him, pauses so long that he almost catches her, but he stops, sighing, and leans against a wall. Another struts by, patting her rump and winking. He follows her to the kitchen and when she bobs out of sight through a black doorway he makes a haphazard dive. Down and down the cellar stairs: they heave his tools after him as he stumbles into a darkness where the putrid odors of mildew and rot scuttle his brain.

It isn't so bad under the house. After a while his eyes accustom themselves to shadows; the reek of time rusting away scares him at first, but finally his hands stop trembling. He is there two days, three, then hunger passes. He doesn't want the grass or trees anymore, doesn't want the touch of a woman nor the busy freedom of the town. He sinks to a subbasement of the spirit, weary, his juices gone. Eventually he picks up his tools and begins a listless duty: he repairs the pipes.

A cavern opens endlessly, crawl spaces and basements linked together, dripping pipes everywhere, and he knows, somehow, that all the houses of the town—even beyond—have the same gaping underbelly. He turns a valve, shutting off the flow in a leaky thicket of pipes;

snips off a section of worn metal, cuts new threading, installs a fresh section. On the cool dirt floor around him lie scattered pieces of material and pipe and the tools of others—ones who were here before him, he supposes—and he is busier now, moving to another problem, a broken grease trap. Over there, waiting, a crimped and useless drain. And here—ha!—a portable radio. It wheezes with the organ music of afternoon soap opera, but he doesn't mind. Give yourself small diversions and pace yourself, he says, and he recalls his old man's patience, how his father wanted to give good service and make his labor an art.

He thinks of women, too, but with emptiness. He works steadily, banging pipes, setting faucets, hearing above his head footsteps and the opening of taps and the flushing of toilets, and the women are on his mind although his body no longer yearns. He sees his hands: wrinkled, as if held under water for a long time or as if very old. And he keeps moving along, through one cave of pipes and puddles after another, on and on, and he becomes contented, settled into his duty and contented, because now he is mending the world and loving its women as they said they wanted love.

Nirvana, Götterdämmerung and the Shot Put

Toby Grogan, like all shot-putters everywhere, was crazy from the beginning. Most of his mammoth life he stood in that small circle, stared transfixed into distant space, pressed an iron ball to his cheek, talked to it, stooped, wheeled, and heaved with all his strength.

He knew it was stupid, but he did little else.

He became a mutterer after his college days, talking to inanimate objects much in the way that he spoke to his iron ball. Also, his back ached. Doorknobs sometimes came off in his hands, too, and he broke chairs when he sat in them. Once in Lafayette, Indiana, he was trying to make love to a willing fan of track and field events, but the bed collapsed and in his ensuing fury he smashed holes in the motel walls with his fists so that Coach Fain had to pay for damages. Grogan spent years going to track meets, back and forth across the country in the cramped seats of buses and planes to the Kansas Relays, the Olympic Trials, the AAU Championships, or the Madison Square Garden Indoor Games. His weight stayed at an even 322 pounds, but sometimes his brain threatened to explode on him. Problems everywhere:

too embarrassed to eat all that he craved in a single restaurant, he often wasted hours taking a meal at two or three establishments; his sponsor, the Greater Chicago Athletic Club, nagged him to return the barbells he carried around the country in his suitcases; and for seven years he kept putting the shot around 70 feet—never quite up to the world's record of 71 feet, 5½ inches. His life, like furniture, kept caving in on him and he turned into a mystic.

"A what?" Coach Fain asked him.

"I read this magazine article on the plane coming back from Denver," Toby explained. "This article about Zen concentration. I began practicing. I began talking to my ball about it."

Abraham Fain was a darkly handsome man who resembled Gregory Peck, but who rejected that image to behave like a worried, nervous, midget track coach—the sort who wore his baseball cap backwards, paced, and continually clapped his hands. His Chicago team—once famous, but needing recruits—consisted of Toby Grogan, a vaulter, two sprinters, and a broad-jumping black who wanted to be listed in all the programs as The Leopard.

"I realize you got problems," Coach Fain observed, trying to restrain himself. "You got that lousy vertebra. You got social problems in restaurants. Also, a mild case of athlete's foot, too many letters from your mama, and sexual desires: I know it all. But I told you, please: put nothing in your head prior to Munich. Remember I especially said keep away from new women or books of any sort."

"This was just a magazine article. It said that in the back of the brain there's this pink fogbank. You climb inside it, so there's no possible chance of outside interference."

Coach Fain rolled his eyes.

The workouts were at Soldier's Field and the Chicago sky was a comforting cobalt blue. Home ground, the Athletic Club just a few blocks away. Workmen, as always, tapped and sawed from someplace behind the stands and from the distant trees and walkways of the surrounding park Toby could hear the voices of birds and children. He tromped over to his familiar ring, fixed the wooden block in place, and hefted his ball. As he kicked his feet, loosening up, Coach Fain's dowdy family, the wife and six plump girls, entered at the far end of the stadium. Toby sighed, thinking how Abe suffered their visits during Chicago practice sessions, and considered the benefits of the somewhat lonely nomadic life. Then he slipped out of his warm-up pants and tried to conjure up a pink fogbank.

"Ball," he whispered, "I'm the big cannon that's going to fire you out of pink smoke today." He then addressed his toes, feet, legs, biceps, forearms, and fingertips by way of urging them, as usual, to do their separate and fluid parts in the effort.

He fought for a mind clear of Coach Fain's loud wife and daughters and all the sounds and distractions of the stadium and nearby park and he struggled against all brute desires and psychic fancies. He didn't even think of food. And for once even his lifelong ambition to heave the iron ball a record distance faded in his gathering concentration. He was beyond ambition and he glimpsed a rolling curtain of fog, stared into it, and took his stance. Down, crouched low, then up, whirling, springing forward, crying, "AAaaaahhmm!" He knew it was one hell of a shot as it came off his fingers.

Eighty feet flat. He measured it twice, three times. Since this was his first and only effort, there was no mistaking that lone indentation out in the dirt where the chalk lines curved and beckoned. He retrieved his ball, walked around that little crater another time, and once more measured its distance back to the circle before strolling over to the coach.

Coach Fain, who was finally disposing of his family with a rigid smile, agreed to stroll across the football field to check Toby's claim. He took two measurements himself and when he had confirmed the accuracy of the metal tape his eyes narrowed and he said, "Okay, Big Tobe, give it another try, huh?"

Toby set himself in the circle, waited, briefly dreamed of the pink fog, and let go again.

"Sixty-six feet, four inches!" Coach Fain called back with a smirk. Then he turned away to watch The Leopard take aim on a nearby sandpit.

Toby went back to his circle holding the ball shoulder-high. He supposed he hadn't allowed the power, the full rapture of the fog, to accumulate properly, so while Coach Fain yelled and the others panted around the track Toby set himself again. A full trance this time: he felt his nerve ends humming, heard voices, watched the fog roll toward him once again. The ball arched into a high orbit beyond his grunt and cry.

Just over eighty feet. He stretched the metal tape to that impossible length once, twice, then, satisfied, he quit for the day.

The room where Toby stayed that spring before the Munich Olympics bore all the tokens of his life. A somewhat narrow mirror on the closet door reflected less than half his full girth while his meager wardrobe peered out from the closet itself: worn seersucker slacks, blue blazer with the shield of the GCAC on the pocket, his English tweed suit (never properly large enough across the back), the fat shoes, and all his sweat clothes. Beneath these, the suitcases stood ready. Near his bed were the barbells and footlocker, its lid thrown open to expose a few pictures glued inside: an old news photo of Randy Matson and last April's Playmate, among others. Beside the portable television set on his bedside table was the packet of letters from his mother in Des Moines, each letter with its plea—entreating him to go into the ministry, to testify against drug abuse like all the other athletes were doing, to come home and farm with his deadbeat father, to marry. The letters gave him indigestion or worse—either heartburn or heartsickness, he once told Coach Fain. The remainder of his room was decorated with loving cups, statuettes, engraved plates and awards topped with gold-plated athletic figurines pointing into space. When traveling, Toby kept the trophies in his footlocker.

That spring in his one-room Chicago apartment he viewed as much of himself as his mirror allowed. He saw a giant, heavy in the heart. Twenty-nine years old now and he had always been a shot-putter. Not that he wanted it especially—though he dreamt, sure, of world records and medals—he just *was* a shot-putter, nothing else. Now he came so close to the mirror that his breath steamed the word which he spoke almost like a kiss. "Mystic," he whispered. Every day he came and scrutinized himself and pronounced that word, and in the nights, bulging with anticipation he really didn't understand, he tossed in his sleep as the bed moaned beneath him. He didn't know why those magnificent throws came only in private. But a great moment, he assumed, was upon him.

Then everybody went to Munich. Coach Fain, his new Olympic coaches on the American squad, The Leopard, the proud and the mighty.

A festive city: the river flashing with summer, all the girls, the pageantry, the Hofbräuhaus decked with pennants. From the very beginning a sense of pleasant destiny came over him and Toby enjoyed himself. Heedless of the curfew posted on the bulletin board at the Olympic compound, he walked along the Maximilianstrasse as if he owned it, mixing with the beer drinkers. And, a curiosity: the Germans, admiring his girth and capacity in the taverns, followed him around. Stout knight, they toasted him. *Mammut.* Some of them—particularly a large blond girl named Karin with heavy breasts bumping beneath her sweat shirt—waited for him outside the Olympic Village in the afternoons after practice, eager to accompany him on his nightly rounds. Or a crowd gathered at the fence in the mornings, peering into the shadows of the new domed stadium, too far away to judge the distance of his efforts, but wondering even then why he seemed to save himself for moments alone, why, alone, his coaches occupied elsewhere, he set himself in a forlorn and deeply melancholy trance, then, coming up, bellowing, erupted with his most magnificent shots.

It was his deep solitude—they presumed it was old-fashioned melancholy because, being German, they *understood* melancholy—which touched them. Also, he performed with an iron ball and they, well, *liked* iron, as they tried to explain to him; there was something definitely medieval about it. But, also, he was just a good fellow, right? They watched him quaff twenty-six liters of beer at the Bräuhallen one night. And he accepted their praise and appreciation, but more: he began to feel strangely at home, at terms with himself and these people and the brooding land and city that lay around the sleek architecture of the new Olympic compound. He talked to his ball about this, pressing it to his cheek and saying, "This crowd likes big things. They want what I want, too: something large and important. That's why they're out there in the mornings looking through the fence." The Olympics, after all: a moment perilous, awful, nearly occult in its majesty.

The week of warm-ups made him a celebrity. A newspaper carried his photo as he posed in the Goetheplatz, a somewhat dreamy expression on his wide face. His admirers multiplied, following him into a shop where he bought a souvenir, an enameled beer stein, for his mother. In the rousing oom-pahing of the Hofbräuhaus he shyly consented to kiss the busty blonde in the sweat shirt and everyone roared approval. They hadn't even seen him throw, for he waved them back to seek the winning rapture of the pink fog on his own, but this didn't matter. *Süss Ungeheuer*, they called him. The Happy Iron Man. Our Toby. They viewed him from a distance as he strode out into the stadium infield, waving coaches away, disdaining measurements. They understood. He was moody, they said, and this was only a sign that his power simmered inside him.

Coach Fain told Toby, "You're not just your usual neurotic self, baby. You're out of it." But when he insisted on measuring a couple of Toby's throws, Toby waved him away.

"Leave me alone, Abe," he said, giving the coach an even stare.

"Allow him a little temperament," Abe finally told the other coaches on the American squad. "Maybe he's got seventy feet in him on a good day." Abe Fain kept his distance, then, and the night after the opening processional he even joined the shot-putter and the entourage for the nightly rounds. "Live and let live," he told Toby. "And, besides, the wife and daughters are back home and you've got some fantastic fräuleins at your elbow, right?"

Karin, the blonde in the sweat shirt, seemed pleased enough with Toby's coach and she and Abe held hands, sang, drank beers, and discussed the phenomenon. "He said a curious thing to me the other night," she confided in Abe.

"What, baby?" he asked earnestly. "Tell the old coach."

"He said he thought—well, this is odd. He felt he had been here before. Long ago, you see. In another life. Did he mention this to you?"

"Never, baby, because I got rules. No books. No women either—but be realistic about that, I say—so especially no books or kooky new ideas. Get what I mean?"

"What muscles," Karin sighed, looking down the table where Toby had agreed to simultaneously arm wrestle two of his admirers.

The night grew rowdy. In high good humor Toby paraded among the tables, one thick arm raised in salute as they chanted, "*Mammut! Mammut!*" Karin, dazed and large and lovely, led the marchers who fell in behind him. Someone pulled the American pennant off the wall and waved it.

The field events initiated the Olympics—as if such promethean heaves and tosses were less important than the later and climactic track events. A shirt-sleeved crowd—Toby's boisterous followers included—gathered early beneath the cool dome of the stadium. The Russian shot-putter was huge, his legs like oaks, and the Turk was big, too, but Toby seemed to dwarf them all; impervious, he stood apart. His expectant admirers called to him, to each other, to the confused Russian, who had been kept from either reading the newspapers or drinking beer. Names were announced on the loudspeaker. Vasily Nikolaivich. Saul Deeter. Jacques Brol. Toby Grogan. Cheers and whistles at the mention of his name.

Except for Toby all the shot-putters gathered close to the circle, standing around or jogging in place or bending to touch their toes. Toby drifted beyond the track, however, and spoke to his ball until an official, a little Austrian all dapper in his Olympic cap and sports coat, ran over and instructed Toby to conform. But Toby demurred. The official wagged a finger up into Toby's face, Toby stood his ground, and the admirers in the stands took this as a sign of exciting things to come and applauded lightly. The Austrian went back and fussed with an American coach, but as the event opened Toby still wasn't in the group.

Alone, a distant gaze in his eyes, Toby took a practice shot; the ball went out in a mighty arch, bringing a gasp from the crowd. It made an ugly hole in the artificial turf where it was clearly not supposed to fall. The little Austrian came back, then, pointing at the crater in the artificial turf and shouting, and from the distant vantage point of the stands he seemed pathetic and funny to Toby's admirers. They slapped their legs.

The loudspeaker then announced Toby's name, but he stayed across the track, unmoving, while a second and third official joined the argument.

Tucking the ball underneath his chin, he mused and spoke to it. He speculated if he somehow might be reincarnated, if once, hundreds of years ago, perhaps, he might have been something, say, as inanimate as a cannon; or a knight, heavier still in a coat of armor and chain mail; or even an actual mammoth, one of those solitary beasts who roamed the Alps and European lowlands, mythic in size, lumbering along, leaving only a few bones and footprints as it shuffled toward its extinction.

"Mr. Grogan," called the voice from the loudspeaker.

"Report for your first effort or forfeit the try." This was repeated in four other languages.

Abe Fain was now with the officials, arguing and gesturing with them in the shadow of Toby's frame as if he weren't there. And Toby mostly wasn't. He was considering that first practice shot. It must have traveled eighty-five feet, he knew, and he wondered where such moments came from, why he could never do such things for the record books, only for his own final knowledge. And while they shouted around him he set himself for another attempt, bending, clearing his head again, dreaming the awesome fog, then letting go. This time Abe Fain caught a sidelong glimpse of the distance, made a quick calculation, and started toward Toby. But they were both consumed in official wrath. Another hole in the artificial turf.

"Here you are not supposed to be!" the red-faced and trembling Austrian spat at Toby. "In der proper place only! There! Throwing in der sand!"

"One more minute and you are disqualified in your first attempt, Mr. Grogan," the voice on the loudspeaker remarked in five languages.

"Big Tobe, baby!" Abe shouted, pushing through the crowd.

Next, two policemen appeared. Following the Austrian's frenzied orders, they proceeded to give Toby harsh instructions, pointing with their nightsticks. Then one of them placed a hand on Toby's arm and found himself whisked up and thrown—not unlike a wrinkled black javelin—until he landed, crash helmet first, in the cinders of the track several feet from the dispute. The second policeman raised his stick, came forward, but was jumped and pummeled by Karin; others followed her from the stands, all the beer drinkers and admirers. Police whistles everywhere. A roar of dismay from those still in their seats and expecting a sporting event. Following this, the announcement that Mr. Grogan is disqualified in the first round, but may have his second and third attempts later. As Karin wrestled the nightstick from the downed policeman, Toby strolled over and picked up his ball. Abe, busy explaining his athlete's temperament to the judges, was clubbed from behind with a low hurdle and fell forward, his baseball cap knocked off. The Austrian was attacked by a flügelhorn. As always, someone thought to have the band play a national anthem, but it was no music anyone recognized so the mayhem continued.

Toby, disdainful of all such distraction, then made what might have been his single greatest heave: he put the ball over the wire fence—the same his admirers had clutched to watch him from afar—and out of the stadium area. Dumbstruck, those left in the crowd broke into applause, but he was gone, stalking off after his ball, which had bounced on a cement runway and rolled downhill beyond everyone's sight. Atop the fence, waving and beckoning, The Leopard called Toby's followers and they streamed out, shoving aside anyone who tried to halt them.

Abe stood up, his nose bleeding, and watched them go.

For a time after that the newspapers charted Toby's travels.

Shuffling across the high meadows and valleys he put the shot, heaving it out ahead, retrieving it, tossing it again, striding after it in a strange journey. When he came close to villages the people came out and watched, giving him and his friends cheese and country wine. The girl and others stayed with him for weeks, then she went back to her job, others dispersed, and still others came to join the trek. An odd band: wandering in a herky-jerky movement all over the continent, into Switzerland, over near Grenoble, then back into Italy, into Yugoslavia. At last he was alone, his followers gone, arching that iron ball into the thin mountain air, mostly staying up in the high country away from the cities, pausing, crouching, putting the shot from his deep trance, passing on. By the time winter arrived the newspapers no longer concerned themselves with him and—as all such stories go—he was never seen again.

Weatherman:
A Theological Narrative

In his seventieth year a strange foreboding comes to Mr. Pollux, the old meteorologist: he begins to understand that he is the God of the Universe.

Certainly, his place is imposing: he is the sole occupant of a gigantic tower, not unlike a fire watcher's perch, high in the Ozark Mountains. The tower is one of nine Mid-America Storm Towers (Operation MAST, project of the National Weather Service) in which skilled weathermen scan the horizons and charts and computer tapes for signs of tornadoes and major disturbances.

In his busy loneliness in the tower, Mr. Pollux eventually faces the vexing evidence: he knows that the weather follows his direction, that it obeys his every projection and mood.

He wonders if his long experience in the business has finally made him especially sensitive or if he is just having a run of lucky coincidence with his forecasts. Yet, testing himself, he finds he can invent the most fanciful or the most oddly precise bulletins which come true down to the last curious detail.

He has two tornadoes bump together, say, near Eureka Springs, Arkansas.

He also tests his mortality by remembering.

Yes, he had a family: parents, long ago, and a sister who married and lives in Toledo.

Also, a favorite nephew, little Cappy.

Cappy came to visit the tower—let's see, he can't quite recall—five summers ago. They went out on the deck which encircles the tower and on the night of the Fourth of July Mr. Pollux produced a fantastic electrical storm: bolts and explosions and everything his nephew could want.

"You're not really making all that thunder and lightning," little Cappy said with a knowing smirk. He was eleven years old that summer.

"Yes I am," Mr. Pollux told him, pointing a finger and making a great fork of electricity.

After his nephew went back to Toledo there were lots of candy and chewing gum wrappers lying around the laboratory and no one ever came to see him again.

Surrounding him are his instruments: hygrographs, radiosondes, microseismographs. His computers rasp and whisper, the radar antenna atop his tower squeaks with every rotation, and the big brass barometer keeps sinking below 29.80.

Every morning he sends up weather balloons.

Twice each day he phones in his reports, which are taken by one of the recording machines of the National Service. Not even a human voice to say thanks.

At night the National Service sends out his bulletins to airports, TV stations, newspapers, corporations, and private meteorologists everywhere.

He imagines millions of people bending forward in

grim reverence before their television sets, listening for tomorrow's sunshine or rain.

You know you're God, he decides, when you're no longer in contact with people, but have magnificent power.

In April he phones his sister long distance, but there has been a freak late-season blizzard up in Ohio and the lines are down.

Annoying, but far away where even the powerful have no control.

He thinks up all of the old theological puzzlers and makes up answers to each one, answers he'd give, say, if anyone ever came to his tower to interview him.

1. If God is good, why does he allow suffering?
   Answer: He is only pretty nice. And whimsical.
2. Is God simply the Prime Mover? Did he create the world and then bow out of its operation?
   Answer: Yes, God retired and was given a gold watch and fob for his services by the eleventh-century theologian Anselm.
3. If God is all-powerful, can he then make a rock so heavy that he can't lift it?
   Answer: Yes, he can make such a rock—and this confuses him. But, then, the essence of the Holy is loneliness and confusion.
4. If God loves mankind, why did he create man finite and even lower than the angels?
   Answer: It is man's lot to sit apart, like an audience.
5. If God is a personal God, where does he sit? And isn't the order in which he is contained greater than he is?
   Answer: A good tower keeper is a daydreamer and all reality is imagination.

Mr. Pollux feels most powerful and important when he makes tornadoes.

This is the great tornado belt of the planet, so everyone expects catastrophe—though not, perhaps, with such frequency as Mr. Pollux provides this spring and summer. Except for a rare cyclone in such faraway places as Pakistan or Turkey, the middle United States has a virtual monopoly on tornadoes. In one weekend in the month of May, Mr. Pollux creates 267 separate twisters in the four-state area.

He feels sorry for the victims, sure, but a first-rate tornado is hypnotic and its vortex is a masterpiece.

Back to the telephone.

Mr. Pollux calls around to the other tower keepers in Project MAST. They're all lonely, eccentric types and most of them have weird, unscientific notions of how things work. The guy in Oklahoma believes that inside dust devils are real devil spirits—mean, dirty monsters just like the Cherokees used to believe in.

"Nuts," Mr. Pollux tells him on the phone.

"I'm writing down my theories in a book," the guy explains, and Mr. Pollux wants to hang up on him.

Mr. Pollux remembers hard, trying to recall as much of normal life as he can. One day he thinks about all the girls and women he has known and about how he enjoyed kissing them. He didn't care much for those open-mouthed, sloppy, overheated kisses, but liked the old-fashioned sort with the lips in tender use. How far back, all this? How long since the last kiss? Straining for recollection, he gets the Roaring Twenties, the Merchant Marine, New Year's Eve in 1949, then primordial images assault his brain and he sees a landscape of volcano, a red sky, the bones of dinosaurs among the ferns and ridges of an ancient jungle.

Animals amble and scurry around the bottom of his tower: bears, raccoons, squirrels, deer.

"My job is statistics!" he calls down to them. "An average of two hundred and thirty-five clear days in a year around here! Stupid piece of information, right?"

He also yells down special weather terms. "Prevailing westerlies!" he calls. "Accluded front!"

Then he goes to sleep and dreams odd nightmares. A strange storm erupts, a rain of fire, and both the forest animals and a mob of people come and rattle his tower trying to climb up. In the dream he comes on TV like the hick weather commentator from Joplin and points with a stick at a weather map. He explains the holocaust to his audience.

"A God who is accessible," he adds, "would not be God."

The computer breaks down and spews out hundreds of feet of tape—data which doesn't even make sense to Mr. Pollux, who puts up with everything. He gathers up the pile of tape, tears it in little bits, goes out on his deck, summons up a strong wind, then pitches the tatters out over the Ozarks like confetti.

Memory, knowledge, everything in the head is a form of madness, Mr. Pollux decides.

The month is June and the horizon is a pavilion of stately thunderheads. He drinks iced tea and contemplates.

God, the mind of all existence, the great perceiver, is a madman. Madness is a holy state. And destruction is the primary form of creation. And God, naturally, as Mr. Pollux knows too well, is suicidal.

In the early autumn Mr. Pollux makes a tornado the size of the city of Wichita, Kansas, and it churns across the helpless prairie, dancing like a fat cobra in the fields. Clouds boil over all mid-America.

Senile and lost in his meditations, Mr. Pollux still won't surrender such ecstasy.

Last mortal efforts.

Mr. Pollux calls the national headquarters in Washington, D.C., and they fail to locate his service record in the Merchant Marine. Honorably discharged, he assures them. Gives his rank, serial number, and ship. Then he calls Toledo. Disconnected. He leaves a message in the recorder at the National Weather Service: "Two-week notice. No more bulletins from me after December." Writes a note, then, on his weekly grocery list and drops it down the mail chute: "Forget the soup this week. Send doctor and priest."

He prepares a great blizzard. Canada is snowed under even as he considers how to phrase his bulletin.

Winds 100 miles an hour, temperatures 60 below, and frozen tidal waves slam into the cities of the Great Lakes. Another Ice Age arrives: fresh glaciers advance, new matterhorns are gouged out of the midwestern plains, the people of Omaha and Des Moines and Denver sealed in the frozen flow, and in the Ozarks the blizzard collides with the lingering zephyrs and a calamity of storm erupts. Mr. Pollux watches from his tower. The skies boom with thunder, ice breaks down the trees, and the animals shudder by, moving south into oblivion.

He sees his death from a great height, far distant, as if he stands beyond the coldest star, his tiny and silly loneliness a sacred and private pain. "Ouch," he tells the cosmos. "Ouch, ouch, ouch." And he flaps his arms against the relentless chill.

Cold: so complete that the metal girders of the tower grow brittle and snap. And the world is as blue and silent as a story in which a single man goes down to death.